BATTLE FOR THE BADGERS

Anthony Masters

For a few more seconds the other two badgers watched the cubs cavorting about. Then the idyll was shattered as a single shot cracked out, and then another. Something hit the side of the sett and the badgers froze. Two more shots followed and they froze again – as did Tim and Flower. They gazed at the badgers in horror. They seemed to be unhurt. But turning to Mr Andrews they saw he had uncoiled himself as if on a spring, and as the badgers dashed for the security of the sett, he launched himself forward with a wild and ragged cry.

Also in the Green Watch series:

Sad Song Of The Whale by Anthony Masters

BATTLE
FOR THE
BADGERS

Book One in the Green Watch series

by
Anthony Masters
Illustrated by Pauline Hazelwood

Hippo Books
Scholastic Publications Limited
London

Scholastic Publications Ltd.,
10 Earlham Street, London WC2H 9RX, UK

Scholastic Inc.,
730 Broadway, New York, NY 10003, USA

Scholastic Tab Publications Ltd.,
123 Newkirk Road, Richmond Hill,
Ontario L4C 3G5, Canada

Ashton Scholastic Pty Ltd.,
P O Box 579, Gosford, New South Wales,
Australia

Ashton Scholastic Ltd.,
165 Marua Road, Panmure, Auckland 6,
New Zealand

First published in the UK by Scholastic Publications Ltd., 1990

ISBN 0 590 76352 0

Typeset by AKM Associates (UK) Ltd., Southall, London
Printed by Cox and Wyman Ltd., Reading, Berks

Chapter One

Tim clung to the rock face with all his might, not daring to look down and certain that he was not going up. His body was frozen. Inside, somewhere near his middle, a little voice cried out in mortal terror, and waves of nauseous fear swept up into his throat. He would *not* go on – whatever they said.

"Get on with it," yelled Seb from below. "You're blocking Flower."

I'm not going anywhere, thought Tim. And I'm damned if I care that I'm blocking Flower. He stole a glance down and gave a little whinny of panic. True, in reality he was only twelve metres from the ground, but it could just as well have been twelve hundred.

"Get *on* with it."

But Tim knew he simply wasn't able to move. He

couldn't speak either.

Flower hissed, "You're in the way."

She was just below him, and was climbing without a line, tucking her feet and hands in the most minute crevices. Tim was on a line and knew he was safe. But he was still too terrified to move.

"What's up with him?" asked Brian.

"Frozen," he heard Seb mutter.

Suddenly Tim hated them all. He hadn't wanted to come here in the first place and he was hating it even more than he had imagined he would. Hating every single moment of it. If only Dad hadn't gone and got himself nicked and ended up inside, and Mum hadn't had a breakdown, he would be happily at home in Peckham. Then he wouldn't be mixed up with Uncle Seb and his kids Flower and Brian. The whole sequence of disastrous events ran through his mind again and again as he clung to the sandstone with numb fingers. Soon he wouldn't feel them, soon they wouldn't support him. Soon he would plunge out on the swinging rope, looking a fool to them all.

"Are you all right, Timothy?" Seb's voice was as cool and precise as ever, without the slightest trace of warmth.

He sneaked another look down. Yes, there he was, as irritatingly critical as ever. Seb stood, legs apart, looking quizzically upwards, his hair slicked down and neatly parted, his lips thin and pencil-like. His cheeks were red, his skin tautly stretched, his eyes dark and piercing. He's like a bird of prey, Tim thought suddenly. A hawk squawking with disapproval.

"Timothy?" The voice was a little sharper.

There was still no reply.

"I'm coming up," he rapped. "Don't move."

Am I likely to, wondered Tim, inwardly cursing his uncle.

Seb began to swarm up the sandstone rock below him. Without looking, Tim knew he was climbing with hands and feet, monkey-like – as Flower had done. Soon he was alongside him. His breath smelt of peppermint, his body of summer seas. That was the extraordinary thing about Seb. He always smelt wonderful.

"What's up?"

Tim shook his head.

"Go on up?"

Tim shook his head again.

"Come on down?"

He nodded.

"OK. I'll tell you what to do. Brian's belaying."

Nod.

"Straight down."

Nod.

"Search for the crevice."

Nod. But still no movement.

"You *have* to move."

Nod.

"Now."

Nod. Still no movement.

"*Now!*"

Tim put a foot down and withdrew it.

"Now!"

Flower was beside him. "It's all right, Tim. Just put your foot down. There's a big crevice here."

This time his foot connected, and the rest was easy.

When he got down and was released from the rope, Tim's knees gave way and he sank to the ground, feeling sick. His legs were shaking and so were his wrists. When he looked round, Seb and Flower were standing watching him in a calm, curious silence. He felt a wimp. He *was* a wimp. Tim wanted to go home. But he was also angry enough to be ready to hurl abuse at them all. This awful superior family who called themselves – who had the damn cheek to call themselves – Green Watch.

"Are we feeling better?"

Flower was small like her father. Brian was taller although he was a year younger than Flower. He was much the quieter of the two. Even now he still hadn't looked up from his book.

"Sorry about that," muttered Tim, blinking back tears of humiliation.

"That's all right." Seb sounded brusque. "You've got the shakes, that's all. Want to have another go?"

Tim shook his head vigorously; he certainly didn't want to have another go. Not if they paid him. Not if they turned a gun on him. But he knew he should and Tim knew that Flower, pushing her straight flaxen hair out of her eyes, would be impatient with him. Flower who had swum with dolphins and climbed

4

high mountains, who had ridden a horse halfway across Mexico – Flower who was capable and didn't like those who were incapable. Like him.

At last Brian put down his book. "You're down," he said in some surprise. "That was quick." Brian was unlike Seb and Flower. He would bury his head in a book for hours at a time, but no one would remonstrate with him at all.

"It's always best to give it another go," said Seb quietly. His eyes were fixed on him. Tim could feel them, steady, penetrating, appraising. Golly, thought Tim, no wonder his wife walked out on him. He was probably the most heartless man in the world.

They walked home in silence, Seb and Flower leading the way, Brian in a dream and Tim behind them, burning with resentment. He could remember his father talking about his brother Seb ages ago. "Real weirdo. Left home at sixteen and started travelling round the world. Always was a funny kid. Never had anything in common with me and Len. Got himself stuck into all these conservation projects. He doesn't like the real world."

But Dad wasn't living in the real world now. He was in the Scrubs for fraud and Len was flat broke, on the dole and living in Balham with his girlfriend. So it seemed that in some funny sort of way, Seb had made it – although it wasn't clear how he made any money. Mum had said that he was paid by a charity to run his Green Watch and that he looked after all kinds of creatures – all the persecuted of the animal kingdom:

5

whales, dolphins, badgers, seals. But so far, although he had been here only a few days, Seb seemed to be filling up his time making life as miserable for Tim as he could. At least, that's how Tim saw it.

It was Whitsun. The weather had been chilly and it had rained most days on the Romney Marsh. But this hadn't stopped him taking them sailing, canoeing and now climbing. Tim had hated them all. He had almost capsized them when it was his turn to take the helm in the dinghy, he had overturned his canoe on the river, had screamed his head off after being temporarily trapped underneath it, and now he had frozen on the rock. Traitorously the bookish Brian had turned out to be a good sailor, a magnificent canoeist, and probably would have shone as a climber if he had cared to try. The thing about Brian was that he wasn't always interested in doing things, but when he did he was superb. Of course Flower had a go at everything and seemed a natural, and Seb – well, Seb could do anything. Blast Seb, thought Tim.

"No!"

Tim barged into Brian. "What's happening?"

"Look." Brian's voice was shaking. Tim looked ahead at the Howards' home – an old windmill they had restored on the marshes. Black smoke was coming from the downstairs windows and was snaking up towards them on the chill wind. Even Tim's worst thoughts abruptly disappeared and he began to run after the Howards as they dashed towards their home.

When they got there, Tim could see bright little

sparks of flame dancing in the kitchen. Jabbing the key into the lock, Seb wrenched open the door and the smoke thickened, billowing out at them.

"Stay out. All of you."

"But Dad –" Brian protested.

"I *said*, stay out. For God's sake."

He disappeared into the murk and they could hear him coughing and gasping.

"I'm going in," said Brian.

"No," warned Flower. "He told us not to."

"I don't always obey him."

"Do so now." Her tone was that of an admonishing schoolteacher.

Tim didn't know what to say. They stood there indecisively. Then they all heard a rushing, squirting sound.

"That's No. 1 Fire Extinguisher," said Flower.

There was a pause and the smoke seemed to shift and sway. Then there came another rushing, squirting sound.

"That's No. 2," said Flower.

"How many have you got?" asked Tim.

"Four. Maybe he won't need to use them all."

The smoke eddied and Seb poked a blackened face out of the doorway.

"You OK, Dad?" Flower's voice was tight with anxiety and Brian looked on the edge of tears.

It was amazing to see them so afraid, thought Tim. He had only seen them as invincible before.

"I'm fine. The fire's out. It hadn't spread far. It's mainly in the kitchen."

"Can we come in?" asked Brian shakily.

"Wait a minute. I don't want anyone damaging evidence."

"Evidence?" muttered Tim. "What do you mean?"

"I mean, we've been fire-bombed."

"What?"

"Someone put a Molotov cocktail through the letterbox," said Seb grimly.

The kitchen was blackened and in some places charred. Smoke still drifted in the air.

"You ought to get some fresh air, Dad." Flower watched with concern as Seb's chest heaved and wheezed as he angrily surveyed the damage. A heat-cracked bottle lay by the letterbox and there seemed no doubt that this was the source of the blaze.

"Whoever did this," pronounced Seb, "means business."

A strange kind of excitement filled Tim and quite suddenly his resentment and distress disappeared. Instead, for the first time since he had arrived, he felt part of the Howards. He looked round the ruined kitchen with a new, observant eye and caught sight of a cracked pane of glass.

"I wonder if they tried to break in first," he said and Seb's eyes followed his to the window.

"It wasn't done before. And it wasn't heat that cracked it." Seb felt the glass. It was quite cool.

"Well, we've got plenty of enemies, Dad," said Brian.

"Don't be so pessimistic," snapped Flower, examining what was left of the kitchen.

"He's right, I'm afraid. The current campaign's certainly not won us much love on the doorstep."

"What is the campaign?" Tim had been longing to ask what they were working on but hadn't dared. His mother's words rang in his ears: "He's barmy, of course. A real crank. Always has been. Anti-hunting, anti-government. And he drags those children in. No wonder Sheila took off."

"It's all a bit domestic at the moment," said Seb. "Most of our projects aren't as close as this. But there's an old friend of mine – a Mr Andrews – who runs a railway museum in an old yard down the road. And in between the tracks – well, you've never seen anything like it, Tim; it's a wilderness of wild grasses and plants and flowers. They've never been sprayed, of course, and because of that it's a paradise for wildlife. Loads of different kinds of butterflies. And a damn great badger sett which has never been disturbed." He laughed. "It's never disturbed because no one goes to the museum now."

"Why not?" asked Tim.

"It didn't pay very well and everything fell into disrepair. But he won't leave the site; he loves the engines too much."

"So *he* isn't the fire-bomber." Tim couldn't help admiring Seb. Here he was in his fire-ravaged kitchen talking quite coolly about railway yards and wildlife and badgers and the peculiar Mr Andrews.

"No." Seb laughed again. "He wouldn't hurt a fly.

9

But he's being persecuted – just like the badgers – and we've annoyed a few people by trying to help him."

"Why's he being persecuted?"

"There's a particularly unpleasant local farmer called Les Johnson who is not only trying to get the Council to agree to gassing the badgers on Mr Andrews' land because he claims they're a health risk to his cattle, but also has his eye on the railway yard so that he can raise a crop of highly profitable caravans there."

"But if it's Mr Andrews' land –" began Tim.

"Trouble is," replied Flower, "it may not be. He bought it off a farmer called Sampson, but Johnson claims that Sampson had no right to sell it – that it was his land."

"So what's happening?"

"It's in the courts," said Brian. "Sampson's dead and it's in the hands of his solicitors. Waiting for a hearing."

"And the trouble is," continued Seb, "that Johnson's been harassing Mr Andrews. He's getting impatient with the long court hold-ups and is trying to get him to accept a ridiculously low figure so that he can buy back what he describes as 'his land'. He's let his truck tyres down, smashed his gate, that sort of thing. And we've been championing Mr Andrews and the badgers and the rest of the wildlife by organizing petitions and involving conservation groups. We don't want an enormous caravan site; we want the yard kept as a natural unspoilt place."

"And you think Johnson'd fire-bomb you?"

"To warn us off. Oh yes, I'm sure this is his work."

"Aren't you going to phone the police, Dad?" demanded Flower impatiently.

"In a minute," said Seb. "But there's nothing we can pin on him."

"Can't they find some fingerprints?" asked Brian.

"What on? A heat-cracked bottle?"

"We *must* do something," said Tim, and with a sudden shock realized he had said "we" as if he was part of Green Watch. With equal suddenness he caught Seb's eye, and for the first time he felt a flicker of warmth between them. And as if in explanation of his earlier brusqueness Seb commented, "I'm not the easiest man to know, Tim. I'm sorry if we've stretched you a bit too far. To be honest, I wanted to know what you were made of."

"Which isn't much," said Tim miserably.

"Rubbish. At least you've tried everything. You've got guts."

"Not enough."

"You'll get 'em. Anyway, it's not guts we're after really. It's – it's being a whole person."

"I don't understand," muttered Tim.

"Experiencing as much as you can," said Seb. "Really living to the full and being aware of things. Do you get me?"

Tim supposed that he did. Seb was about to go on but Flower interrupted. "When Dad says he's not the easiest man to know I can tell you he really means it. He puts off more people than I've had hot dinners."

"They all think he's a weirdo," said Brian. "We get

11

hell at school. Lucky he taught us karate."

"Karate?" Tim was amazed. Was there no end to Seb's talents?

Seb grinned. "I'm only a red belt. Still, it's got me out of a few scrapes."

"I thought it was animals you protected," said Tim.

"Yes." Seb grinned again. "But a lot of humans get in the way."

"What are we going to do now, then?"

"Phone the police and tighten our defences."

"And then?" asked Flower.

"And then we're going to get some evidence on Johnson and put him away for a good long time."

"Easier said than done, Dad." Brian was right to be pessimistic, Tim thought.

"I'm going to have that guy," said Seb and there was ice and fire in his voice. "I'm really going to have him." Then his concentrated look disappeared and he smiled at Tim in a conspiratorial sort of way. "You're part of Green Watch now, Tim, whether you like it or not."

And in the smoke-blackened kitchen, with the acrid smell of burning still in his nostrils, Tim felt a great surge of elation. He had been tested and accepted, and it was almost as if this extraordinary, cold yet fiery man had offered him blood-brotherhood. It was a wonderful feeling. Then Tim looked down at the heat-broken bottle and felt the first chill of fear. But his spirits soared above it. For the moment.

Chapter Two

The police were talking to Seb in the kitchen while Tim, Flower and Brian sat in the big main room of the windmill feeling out of it, pretending to watch television while thinking their own separate thoughts. Tim was particularly sad: the policeman reminded him of another policeman who, weeks ago, had come to question his own father and had eventually taken him away.

Then Flower said, "I know what you're thinking."

"Eh?" Tim was taken completely by surprise.

"You're thinking about your dad."

"How did you know?" he asked defensively.

"The police hanging around?"

He nodded.

"You don't mind me talking about it?" asked Flower.

"She's very nosey," said Brian. "She always got her nose in something."

"Shut up. Dad said we shouldn't hide it."

"But not ram it down his throat."

"I'm not, am I?" For the second time in a few hours Tim was moved by the unexpected. How weird these people were, really weird. First of all they were steely and demanding. Now the ice had melted they were full of concern. But it wasn't warm concern: it was fiery concern, as fierce as the flames that Seb had had to battle with in the kitchen. Then he had his most powerful insight of all, but he was sure that it was the truest. They were fire and ice, these Howards. Was that being the whole person Seb had spoken of?

"You're not," said Tim. "It helps to talk about it. I was just thinking," – his voice suddenly shook with emotion – "their coming here reminds me of when he was taken away."

Tears ran down his face and he felt bitterly ashamed. But Brian got to his feet, dropped his book and came over to him. Flower knelt down at his feet and clasped his knees. Tim continued to cry.

"Let it out," said Brian commandingly.

"Boys don't cry," said Tim through his sobs.

"Then they're fools," replied Brian sternly.

"Everyone should cry," asserted Flower. "Never bottle anything up. Dad cries."

"Seb?"

"Yes. Quite a lot actually."

"On the rock face?"

She sighed. "He did once. It was when Mum left."

She's only the same age as me, thought Tim. And yet she acts like – like, well not a grown-up exactly. Just very different.

When Seb came back into the circular living-room that he had constructed inside the windmill, he looked worried.

"What's up, Dad?" asked Flower.

"Local police – complete idiots."

"Won't they help?"

"Non-starters. CID are coming but they don't hold out much hope. Any local enemies, he asks. Of course I told him all about Johnson and then he asked me what evidence I had. I said was going to find it, and he told me to be careful."

"Careful?" Flower was furious.

"Careful about taking the law into my own hands. As if I was going to!"

"All right, Dad. Calm down," said Brian. "You probably look the type who would – I mean, they think we're troublemakers anyway. What do you expect?"

"That's because of the peppermint trails we laid for the hounds to follow – away from the horses," Flower explained to Tim, who was wondering if Seb could see any tearstains. Then he suddenly knew that it really didn't matter if he did. "It was brilliant. They couldn't find them for ages, and then they found us and the landrover and tried to overturn it and –"

"All right," said Seb, looking at the round-eyed Tim. "Don't put him off. We only break the law when we have to – when it's right to." He looked round the room. "What worries me is if he tries this again, the whole lot could go up. And that would be very hard to bear." Amazingly, there was a sob in his voice. Flower had been right.

The circular living-room, of course, was special but because everything had been so upsetting, Tim had not allowed himself to take it in. But now he did, seeing it through Seb's eyes as well as his own. It was more oval than circular, he supposed, and reminded him of a ship's cabin. There were photographs of all kinds of animals against all kinds of backgrounds; heavy Shetland seas, polar regions, a Californian surfing beach, an Indian canyon, part of a desert – it seemed there was nowhere where Green Watch had not been. And elsewhere on the walls were maps, bookcases jam-packed with books, ships in bottles, models of ships, paintings of the desert, a ship's figurehead, a host of model windmills, more books, more everything. It was a riot of experience and colour and light.

"I couldn't bear it," Seb repeated.

"We'll have to get one, then," said Brian.

"We can't. We travel too much."

"Borrow one."

"That'd be no good."

"What are you on about?" asked Tim.

"A dog," said Flower sadly. "Dad's right. When we're out of school we're usually travelling somewhere. It would be cruel to have a dog."

"What about Rusty, then?" asked Tim.

"Rusty?"

"Our dog. Well, Dad's dog really. He's at home. He'd like to come down – and he's an Alsatian. He's a bit old but Dad always said he was a good guard dog."

Seb went up to Tim and grasped his shoulders. "Are you sure?"

"Sure I'm sure." He had never felt so proud. Not only was he accepted but he had something – someone – to contribute. Rusty.

"One thing," said Seb.

"What?"

"He wouldn't survive another fire bomb."

Tim nodded. He didn't want to expose Rusty to danger. And anyway, would Mum let him come?

"But I tell you what." Seb was purposeful again, no longer vulnerable. "We *can* have Rusty, but only if we build a stockade."

"A stockade?" Flower laughed. "This isn't Treasure Island, Dad."

"Isn't it? It's my treasure island. And should be yours. And I *am* going to build a stockade. Remember that pile of fencing I've got stored in the shed?"

"That's for sheep," said Brian.

"Well, sheep are out for a while. Sorry – I know you wanted them. But they'll have to wait, OK?"

"OK, Dad. But will it be high enough?"

"It was meant for a windbreak. Yes. But I know

where I can get some more, and it's cheap. We'll get it sorted out tomorrow. And then if we have Rusty *inside* the stockade, we'll be able to turn the windmill into a fort." He was fire now – all fire.

"But Dad," interrupted Flower, "we can't have Rusty for ever."

"This situation won't go on for ever," Seb said quickly. "In fact I intend to stop it within the next few days."

"How?" asked Tim.

"We'll all do it. What we have to do is to draw the enemy's fire – and then jump 'em."

"You mean, get Johnson out in the open?" Flower's eyes were sparkling.

"I want to think it out." Seb looked at his watch. "It's after nine. You lot should be in bed. I'll wait up for the CID. They should be here soon."

"Shouldn't someone be on guard?" asked Tim. "I'll volunteer."

"Thanks," said Seb. "But I need some thinking time. We'll launch the battle plan at breakfast. Get some sleep. And Tim –"

"Yes?"

"Welcome to Green Watch."

Tim slept fitfully that night. He dreamt dreams of high adventure. In each dream he was with the Howards; in each dream he saved them from certain death – whether it was in a desert, sea, or river, or on a mountain top. He was their saviour, and as each rescue was daringly pulled off, they came to depend on him more and more. Towards dawn he had more-or-less taken on Seb's role; he was now his trusty lieutenant as they battled their way through bandit country in an obscure South American state. Tim was just fighting his way through a narrow canyon at the head of which was Seb, just about to be lashed behind a wild stallion, when he was awoken by a light, sure touch on the shoulder.

"Who's that?" He rolled over to see Seb standing over him in a tracksuit.

"Fancy a run?"

"A run?" Tim felt totally exhausted after his shallow sleep and wild dreams. But he nodded obediently.

"Brian's going to get the breakfast and start cleaning up the kitchen and Flower wants to catch up with some holiday homework. So . . ."

"I'll be down."

"Good for you."

Seb hurried out, leaving Tim to groan, pull the covers over his head and then tumble reluctantly out of bed.

It wasn't a jog; it was a real run. They darted along the dyke that led from the back of the windmill, over the fields and down towards the sea, which lay winking blue in the early morning sunshine. A track ran alongside the beach and it seemed to go on endlessly towards a clear, sparkling horizon. Tim was quite a good runner at school, and for the first ten minutes he was able to keep up with Seb's easy jog.

Then he began to find it relentless, and after a while he realized that he was beginning to slip behind. Seb slightly eased his pace, and the track was smooth, but Tim still found the going too much for him. All his shame and inadequacy of the previous days returned to him as he got slower and slower, ending doubled up on the track, his breath coming in painful gasps.

"Sorry."

"What are you sorry about?"

"I'm not keeping up."

Seb looked as expressionless as he had when Tim had frozen to the rock. Yet now he didn't feel he was hostile – just waiting.

"I'm sorry," he gasped again.

"Stop saying that."

"Sorry." Tim was still doubled up.

"Tim –"

Gradually he drew himself up. "I'm better now."

"Look, it's mind over matter."

"What?"

"It's the way you're thinking." Seb's tone was very quiet.

"How do you mean?"

"Well, if we can control our minds, then our minds can control our bodies."

Blimey, thought Tim, is he a hypnotist as well? "You mean – what *do* you mean?" Tim was still panting.

Seb laughed. It was about the first time Tim had ever heard him laugh and he got quite a shock. It was a barking sound and seemed to echo over the flat seascape. "I'm only talking about willpower. You don't think well enough of yourself, Tim. Say to yourself: I'm going to run and go on running for ever. Don't let that little voice inside you say you're not. Think running; bury your mind in your body. Believe in your body."

Bury your mind in your body? That sounded good to Tim. Too often his brain told him he couldn't do something, that he would fail. Like on the rocks yesterday.

"OK," said Tim. "I'll try."

"Good. Let's start at a gentle peace."

"Right."

And they did – and Tim didn't think. He lived only for the motion of his body.

"Keep it gentle," said Seb.

He did, and in the end it was more like floating than running. They seemed to go on for miles instead of only half a mile. The landscape, the beach, the sea – all were a gentle blur. Only the motion of his legs and arms was important; it seemed to match his breathing, to be part of it.

"OK. Let's have a sit," said Seb.

"Fine."

Tim sat down, breathing quickly but not nearly as unevenly as before.

"How do you feel?"

"Great."

"Remember, bury your mind."

"Yeah, I will remember that. It feels good."

"It's a wonderful feeling. No mental stress – just

physical elation." He smiled at Tim as they sat there on the pebble ridge. "I love this place; I feel free here." Seb gazed out at the calm sea. There was a film of haze on the horizon, making everything slightly mysterious. Slowly it began to drift towards them. "Wherever we go, I yearn for this place."

"Have you always run Green Watch?"

He laughed. "Lord, no. I used to be a journalist. Crime reporter, actually. Hated every moment of it. Always loved animals and birds, but no one wanted much reporting on them. Not newsworthy enough. Then I did a story on a nuclear power station up North. Seems a bloke had been murdered because he found out something – I don't know what but there'd definitely been some kind of leak. A few days later I was shown some birds that had been contaminated. It was awful – what it had done to them. So I threw up the job and worked for a little campaigning anti-nuclear magazine, which naturally went broke. My wife was going crazy. We lost our house in Canterbury; and I was broke too. Then I had the Green Watch idea. That's when Sheila walked out."

He paused and was silent for so long that Tim wondered whether he should break the silence or not. But on reflection he decided that it was very important he didn't.

Abruptly Seb began again. "I got some backing from a charity and then I got sponsorship. Sometimes it drives me crazy raising the money. I'm no businessman. But I've managed so far. We've got enough to do some work on whales in the Falklands in a few months. The kids'll have to miss a bit of school but I'm not worried about that. This is much more educational." His voice was firm.

If only I could go, thought Tim. He wondered if he would ever be invited.

"What about the badgers?"

"Are they sponsored?" Seb laughed. "No, they're not seen as important enough. It's a back-door job, this one. Ever since we've had the mill – and that's two years now – we've been aware of the problem. But now we've got to do something about it."

"It's a fantastic place – the mill."

"It might work again some day. I bought it derelict and we three did the conversion ourselves. It was cheap, but a hard sweat. They're good kids, those two – even if Brian spends half his time buried in a book and Flower spends all hers bossing me about!" He grinned but his face had that strangely vulnerable look again. Tim suddenly realized how much Seb depended on Flower and Brian.

"OK. On your feet, and remember: bury your mind."

Tim got up and ran lightly back along the track with Seb. He managed to bury his mind and the floating sensation returned.

"Well, Dad?"

"Mm?"

They were sitting over breakfast and Tim felt a glow of well-being.

"Have you thought of anything?" asked Brian. "What's the battle plan?" He had made an amazingly good job of clearing up the kitchen. Much of the woodwork was charred but most of the smoke stain had gone. Miraculously, the stove had escaped and the electrics were functioning. They had obviously caught the fire bomb in its early stages.

"Wait a minute," said Tim suddenly. "If that fire bomb – or Molotov cocktail or whatever it was – did so little damage, it can't have been chucked in long before we came."

"Either that or it had been smouldering," said Brian.

Feeling slightly deflated, Tim wondered if he had said something silly.

"Either's possible." Seb was quick to intervene. "The CID were here till late, poking around and asking how many enemies we had. I said most of the fox-hunting community for starters and they went away looking defeated." He laughed. "Then I had my think, and the battle plan is this –" He pulled a notebook out of his tracksuit pocket.

1. *Get Rusty*
2. *Build stockade*
3. *Alert Mr Andrews*
4. *Catch Johnson red-handed*
5. *Get him arrested*

"There you are," said Seb. "I want to wrap this up in a few days."

For the first time Tim was taken aback rather than overawed. There was a curious childishness to the list – as if it had been written in comic strips with balloons – and Seb had made a very hard job sound dead simple. But there was no such reaction from Flower or Brian. They took it all as a matter of course.

"You mean catch him harassing Mr Andrews – or us – or both?" asked Flower.

"I want to catch Johnson before he does any real harm. But you have to realize we're baiting a trap."

"And we're all the bait," said Brian.

"Want to phone your mum, Tim?" asked Seb. "I can go and pick Rusty up while you help build the stockade."

"All right," said Tim, still not knowing whether she'd agree to the idea. Suppose she wouldn't? Then he would have let them all down.

"Mum?"

"Yes?" Her voice was weak. Since her breakdown and Tim's departure Mrs Howard had had her sister staying with her. She was quite unable to plan for the future and lived only for the day.

"It's Tim."

"How are you, darling?"

"I'm fine."

"They're not too weird for you, are they?"

"They're great."

"I was really worried about your going down there. God knows your dad's in bad enough trouble, but I remember Sebastian as a terrible –"

Tim cut in quickly. "Mum –"

"Mm?"

"Could I have Rusty down here?"

"Rusty?"

"Yes."

"But why?"

"I'd like to have him with me."

"So you *are* lonely."

"No."

"I might have known."

"Mum, I said no. I'm not in the least. Honest." He wracked his brains for a reason; he certainly couldn't give the real one. "We go for such long walks and they haven't got a dog and I thought Rusty couldn't be getting much exercise and –" He broke off.

"Exercise? I can't give him much of that. How can I? The way I feel."

"I'm not blaming you, Mum."

"Well, I must admit he's a big dog to have around and when I go and see your dad he's always on about exercise and I don't see how on earth I can –"

"How is Dad?" He had been wanting to ask at the beginning but hadn't dared in case she launched into another tirade against him, which he couldn't have borne.

"He's all right. Looked pale."

Well, thought Tim impatiently, he's hardly likely to get a tan in prison.

"Sent you his love. He's writing. Got your letter." She paused and Tim knew she was thinking about something else. "This Rusty business –"

"Yes, Mum?"

"I suppose you *could* give him more exercise."

"He'd run miles every day."

"He's getting on."

"It'll do him good."

"Who'd pick him up?"

"Seb's offered."

"*Uncle* Seb to you."

"Uncle Seb," repeated Tim dutifully.

"I'm not sure that I want to see him. What with all this –"

"Auntie Peg could hand over Rusty."

"We'll see."

"But he can come?"

"Yes. Might do him more good than –"

"Thanks, Mum. Seb – Uncle Seb – will ring with the details."

"Tell him to talk to Auntie Peg. I'll get her to answer the phone for a bit."

"OK. I'd better go now."

"Tim – are you all right?"

"Course I am. Take care. I'll ring soon. Bye."

Tim put the phone down triumphantly and darted back into the living-room.

"Battle Plan. Phase One. Rusty," he announced proudly. "Completed."

A cheer went up from Green Watch.

Chapter Three

Seb, having phoned Auntie Peg, set off to collect Rusty just before lunch, leaving Brian, Flower and Tim to manhandle the heavy fencing out of the shed and then start digging a trench to sink it in. It was long, hard, arduous work and Tim found Brian and Flower not only much more competent than he was, but far stronger. But Seb's words kept coming back to him – "bury your mind in your body" – and he tried and it seemed to work again well enough.

They had a snack lunch and laboured on until about three. The afternoon was golden – warm and sunny – and all three dug in companionable silence. Brian and Flower seemed to know exactly where the ditch should go, and as far as Tim knew they had received very little guidance from Seb. He obviously trusted them implicitly, thought Tim. It was a far cry from his relationship with his mother. She hadn't trusted him or his dad in anything, and worst of all she had been quite right.

They were having a brief rest when the phone rang. Flower went in to answer it, and when she came out, she looked white and shocked.

"It's Mr Andrews. He's in trouble."

"What's up now?" asked Brian.

"Someone took the brake off one of his locomotives, and it's gone through an aviary."

"A what?" Brian seemed transfixed.

"A giant bird cage, you idiot," she snapped.

"I know what an aviary is."

"He wants Dad, but he won't be back for a couple of hours."

"Damage?"

"Yes, the owner's furious."

"Johnson again."

"Could be vandals. We should go to him."

"You go with Tim. I'll stay on guard here. Just in case."

Flower hesitated. "OK." Then she said, "Will you be all right?"

"Of course," he said impatiently.

"I'll stay if you like," muttered Tim. But he didn't want to. He wanted to go with Flower.

"Go," said Brian. "Give him what help you can."

They cycled across the marsh to the railway yard. Tim borrowed Brian's bike, which seemed to have a confusing number of gears, very sharp brakes and an extremely narrow saddle. It was a twenty-minute bumpy ride down some badly surfaced B roads across the flat countryside, until they came to what looked like a derelict bus station. It was huge and gaunt, with half its steel roof gaping open and grass growing over a cracked forecourt. A rusting petrol pump was surrounded with piles of old scrap metal and what looked like dozens of wooden crates. Down by the side ran a small, rutted lane.

They bumped and ground their way over the uneven surface that led through a tunnel of dark trees which closely overhung the lane. It was sinister and there was a dry, used-up feeling to it. The carcass of an old van was sprawled across a ditch and an old bedstead hung crazily from a tree. A little further on, a bleak little wood was trunk deep in litter, including the front cabin of a truck, a mysterious number of old prams and bikes and what looked like the back wheels of some kind of tractor. It was a graveyard of machines and domestic appliances and its sombre atmosphere oppressed them both.

"It's amazing – it's so horrible," said Tim.

"Dad calls it Forbidden Earth. Sometimes he even calls it the Cursed Land."

"I can see what he means."

"But once we're through it, it's like going into the past."

At first, on coming out of Forbidden Earth, as Tim was always to refer to the dark lane, it seemed that little had changed except the dismal drama of the scenery. For they had ridden into industrial ruins of such starkness that Tim gasped. Five storeys above him, in ruined, crumbling, moss-ridden brick, loomed a huge building, not unlike the bus station but a much more commanding structure. Most of the upper part had fallen away and only a brick finger was left, pointing balefully up at the sky. The windows were dark gashes and huge doors, partly wrecked, gave way to one single railway line that ran out towards the marshes.

"It's like a cathedral," said Tim.

"Yes," said Flower. "We're out of Forbidden Earth, and into Mr Andrews' world."

"Blimey," said Tim. "I can see what you mean."

They were cycling up to a barred gateway with wire at its top and a huge pipe.

"What's that?" he asked.

"The doorbell – or the alarm. Pull the strap or try to climb the gate and it'll start sounding off. I'll show you."

But Tim had eyes only for what he could see over the gate and through the broken door of a shed. The most enormous locomotive stood there, giant-like in dark green with a waiting air, and next to it he could make out the shape of another. Beside the huge engine shed, but just short of it, was another building from which stretched another single line. There was a signal box, highly decorated, and signals, lots of old tin advertising slogans, and scattered everywhere, either on broken concrete foundations or hunched together along an old arm of a platform, were dozens

31

of old cars, some almost veteran, others Austins and Morrises from the fifties. There were also old jeeps, a wartime ambulance, caravans and a truck that looked as if it had once served as a snack bar. The result was breathtaking and hard to absorb. It was bizarre and very haunting in the fading light.

Flower dismounted from her bike and pulled the cord. It gave a wailing factory hooter sound which seemed to emphasize the time-warp atmosphere they were about to plunge into. The gathering twilight softened the shapes of the old cars until they began to look like a crouched and waiting convoy, about to set off on some romantic adventure at the end of the finger-like railway lines.

The wailing died away and a massive dark shape emerged from one of the caravans. Striding towards them was one of the fattest men Tim had ever seen.

"Mr Andrews."

"Flower – I need your dad."

"I know. He'll be along soon. But can't I do anything?"

"Maybe." He had a highly educated voice which gave a dignity to his enormous bulk. Mr Andrews opened the gate and Tim could see that he had a sagging, handsome face with a walrus moustache, beard and long hair that hung right down over his shoulders. He was wearing a filthy boiler suit that smelt, not unpleasantly, of engine oil.

"She was in the dip. I was cleaning her and went for a cup of tea. Someone took her brakes off – and they'd have to have known what they were doing."

"Johnson?"

"He wouldn't be able to find them. He'd still be clambering all over the footplate when I got back."

"Which one?"

"Bessie."

"Oh dear, I'm so sorry."

"She's gone through this aviary. Luckily it was empty for cleaning. Real miracle, that. But it's done terrible damage."

"Let's go and see."

"It's the owner. I told him Bessie had been sabotaged, but he wouldn't listen. And he called the police – and they won't believe me – and I'll need a crane to pull her out – and –"

"Let's go and see," repeated Flower.

Looking hunched and dejected, Mr Andrews turned back to the engine shed.

"This is Tim. He's a member of Green Watch."

"Hi, Tim," he said, stumbling along, a huge flapping wall of a man who didn't look back.

"Don't worry," said Flower. "He's really upset."

"I'm not," replied Tim. But he was pleased she'd included him. It was now almost dark and there were bats flying about in the gloaming. There was also a sweet scent of meadow grass and herbs.

"We'll have to use this," said Mr Andrews.

They had paused by the track alongside a peculiar-looking truck with a handle at one end.

"It's a linesman's car. Climb aboard." They sat down on two hard iron seats at the front while Mr Andrews cranked from behind, and soon they were speeding along the track. Gradually the derelict cars were left behind and they briefly travelled past a tangled thicket and then sped out into a meadow which smelt so beautiful that Tim said, "Blimey."

"What's that?" asked Mr Andrews, toiling away behind them. "What'd he say?"

"He says he thinks the smell's amazing," translated Flower.

"Ah, meadowsweet. Well, it's my paradise. My threatened paradise. You can smell it, young man? Well you should do, it should smell wonderful. Thirty years and never been sprayed. You should see my butterflies, my wild flowers, my herbs. You should just see them." Then he became cynical. "You won't see them for long, though."

"There's someone there."

"What?"

"I saw someone," insisted Tim.

Mr Andrews braked the trolley and it came to an immediate halt, practically shooting them out of their seats.

"Where?"

"There."

But there was nothing now. Nothing stirred at all.

"You sure?" asked Mr Andrews.

"Thought I was."

"Better carry on. See the damage. Won't be long," he muttered. He cranked up the trolley again and they sped off into the scented night.

The locomotive was vast – a great black monster of a

thing. Once they had got down off the trolley and walked round, Tim could see her name standing out in gold relief: QUEEN ELIZABETH I – Bessie to Mr Andrews. She was halfway off the track, had pushed her way through a pair of buffers, through what looked like a garden shed, and beyond that lay the shattered aviary. A spotlight lit the devastation and the only undamaged thing seemed to be Bessie.

"Mr Fanshaw," said Mr Andrews.

He was an elderly man with pebble-lensed glasses. His eyes seemed to glint manically behind them as he fiddled amongst the debris.

"My young friends," said Mr Andrews by way of explanation.

"Who?"

"Green Watch."

"Good God, is this your conservation group? They're only kids."

"There is a father."

"Where is he?"

"On his way."

"I don't want to see him. I've phoned my solicitor, and my insurance company. I don't want to see some environmental whatsit. And I advise you to speak to your own solicitor – your own insurance company. And by the way, I want to know something." His voice ended on a high trembling note.

"Yes?" asked Mr Andrews tentatively, while Tim watched Flower trying not to giggle.

"When are you going to get your engine out of my back garden?"

"Er –"

"You need a crane."

"Yes."

"Get a crane then!"

"That could be tricky," said Mr Andrews quietly.

"And why is that?"

"I don't have one."

"Hire one."

"Can't afford –"

"You mean – you mean your engine's staying here? My shed? My aviary? My birds are in temporary accommodation. In *my* house. Do you understand, you silly, silly man? My house is full of birds."

Flower snorted with laughter and then unsuccessfully tried to turn the sound into a bout of coughing. Tim stood there, staring at her in horror. Surely this old man was going to blow his top any minute.

"Of course I'll do everything I can to remove my locomotive."

"I want it out of here by tomorrow morning."

"Well, really I don't –"

"Fix it."

"But –"

"I said, fix it!"

He left them abruptly and Mr Andrews stumped away, followed by Flower and Tim.

"I'll never do it," he almost sobbed. "How can I get a crane? I can't even pay the telephone bill."

"What about the insurance?" asked Flower.

"I don't have any."

"What?"

"Well, a bit. But not enough. They've gone and done me now. That Johnson –"

He got back on the trolley and they joined him. As he yanked the handle up and down it was as if he was stretching Mr Johnson's neck. They shot back along the straight line, silhouetted in the dark like figures from another age.

"Well, there's no one been around," said Mr Andrews, fresh from an inspection of the engine shed. "Want a cup of tea?"

"I wonder what's happened to Dad?" Flower looked at her watch. "It's nearly nine. He's very late."

"Perhaps we should go back," said Tim. "No. Wait," he hissed. He thought he could see movement again. Or were his eyes playing tricks and making a fool of him again? He just couldn't be sure.

But Flower had seen it now. "Someone's there. By the old engineers' office." It was a ruined building stuck to the side of the engine shed. "Someone's in there," said Flower.

"I'll go," said Mr Andrews softly.

"And we'll go with you."

"Creep," he whispered. They crept as best they could, although it was hard going over the rough concrete. Whoever it was seemed to be busily engaged in doing something in the small engineers' office. They could see a bent back and the pale moonlight picked out a thin pair of shoulders.

Slowly they crept on. Mr Andrews put a finger to his lips, went up to the door and with a sudden, gusty roar of anger, kicked it open.

A tall, thin boy of about fourteen was standing in the room. It was very shadowy but in the moonlight they could see a sleeping bag on an old mattress.

"Luke!" said Mr Andrews. "Why didn't you say you were coming?" His tone was suddenly friendly.

"Saw you buzzing about. Heard what had happened. Thought you'd be too busy – should have helped."

"But now you're here – have a cup of tea?"

"No, thanks. I'm too knackered. I'll just get some kip."

"This is Luke," said Mr Andrews vaguely. "He's one of my lodgers."

"Lodgers?" Tim gazed round the untidy little room, which was covered in dust and packed with broken furniture. It didn't seem much of a place for lodgers. Then he noticed other old mattresses, other sleeping bags, wedged amongst the debris. But he didn't like to say any more.

As they were walking back to Mr Andrews' caravan, there was a screech of brakes outside the gate and Seb bounded out of the landrover and rang the siren. Hurriedly Mr Andrews unlocked the gate and let him in. As he did so, the siren faded away.

"I don't want to upset the neighbours with the noise," he said, speaking to Tim for the first time. "But I *must* have a warning system."

Upset, thought Tim. He must drive them half out of their minds. Mr Andrews, with his sirens and runaway locomotive, did seem to be high in nuisance value.

"Had a flat on the way back," said Seb. He whistled, and Rusty jumped out of the back. Tim was overjoyed. In all the excitement he had forgotten what Seb was doing and here, miraculously, was Rusty in all his usual, loving agitation.

"He's a nice dog," said Seb. "Let's give him a run and have a talk."

They sat outside the caravan while Rusty explored and Mr Andrews made tea and told them about the impossible problem of the derailed train.

"It's all right. I know a crane driver who watches birds on the marshes. I'll ring him." Seb went to the telephone, had a brief conversation and returned.

"He'll do it."

Mr Andrews' eyes nearly popped out of his head. "He'll what?"

"Do it. Tomorrow morning."

"But what's it going to cost?"

"Nothing."

"But – but –"

"Don't worry about it. He's a friend. He understands about this place. You're not alone, Alan."

Tears flooded into Mr Andrews' eyes and he turned away. "I can never thank you enough."

"You can thank me when we've nicked Johnson. As it is, I don't know which place we should be guarding – yours or mine."

Just before they went home, Seb looked at his watch and said to Mr Andrews, "Badger watching tonight?"

"I always do. It keeps me going."

"Ever done that, Tim?" he asked.

"No."

"Want to?"

"You bet."

"Not too tired?"

"Course not," said Tim defensively and Seb grinned.

"Then why don't you and Flower stay for a bit and take a look; then come home on your bikes and I'll have a good supper ready. I suppose I'd better take Rusty – he seems to quite like me. I must relieve poor old Brian."

Tim walked with him to the gate which Mr Andrews had mercifully opened without sounding his siren.

"What does he mean by his lodgers?" he said. "There's one here now."

"They don't help either," said Seb. "Who did you see?"

"A boy called Luke."

"Oh, him. There's about half a dozen of them all told. They're kids who get chucked out from home or run away or whatever, kids maybe who would end up sleeping rough in London. Instead they bunk off to the railway yard for a few nights and he lets them sleep in the old engineers' office. Police have been down here a couple of times and they've told him not to have them on the premises. He always says he won't. But it's funny how old mattresses and sleeping bags are always lying around in that office. He's a good man, Andrews: child-like himself, I s'pose. Alan used to be an architect with a big house in Woolwich, you know. But he gave it all up to play trains. And cars. He loves all this transport so much: the cars and trains are like children to him. And the lodgers? Well, they're just fellow sufferers, I s'pose."

Seb walked over to his landrover and grinned at him. "I see the stockade's going well."

"We were all digging the ditch when we had to come down here."

"Brian's done well. He's bashing on. Tim –"

"Yes?"

"It's good to have you here. Sorry about the hassles. Enjoy the badgers – and don't be too long."

Tim walked back to the others feeling totally aglow. Perhaps he was tired but he felt almost heady with emotion. As he passed the engineers' office he caught sight of a fleeting movement and saw the boy Luke watching Seb drive off. He was watching him very intently, so he couldn't be as tired as he had made out. Then he turned, saw Tim watching him, and ducked down. Tim walked on thoughtfully.

"Ready?"

They had been sitting for an hour in Mr Andrews' stuffy caravan and Tim was already feeling quite sleepy.

41

"OK," said Flower. "Let's go."

"Are you sure we're being fair on Brian?" asked Mr Andrews.

"Yes," said Flower firmly. "He was with you all last weekend while I had to paint the bathroom. He's done enough badger watching to last him a lifetime."

"Right," said Mr Andrews hastily. "Now I'll just give you a few tips, shall I, Tim?" Tim suddenly realized that Mr Andrews was actually quite scared of Flower. "First of all, if you want to watch badgers you have to swallow yourself."

"Swallow yourself?" said Tim in amazement.

"Pretend to. So that you're on the inside looking out – as if your body's an immovable shell and you're peering through it. I know it sounds easier said than done, but it's possible if you really relax."

"To swallow yourself?"

"To imagine you have. Then you won't sneeze or fidget or swallow or –"

"Breathe?" asked Tim.

"Shallow breathing only," said Mr Andrews. "Please."

They walked slowly through the herb-scented thickets and then Mr Andrews gestured to them to stop, pointing at a little copse some hundred yards from the railway line.

"It's just beyond the copse. So we mustn't talk again. Any questions?"

"Has Johnson been after them?" asked Tim.

"He won't get on my land again. It was before I had the gate and the siren. Couple of months ago I found him in there with some other men and that diabolical equipment. Said they were bringing disease to his cattle."

"And they don't," said Flower, just in case Tim thought Mr Andrews was covering up. "It's scientifically proven."

"Of course," replied Tim hurriedly. He wanted to believe Mr Andrews anyway, but the latter obviously had a habit of sweeping everything before him – and anything he didn't want to know to the side.

"I managed to warn them off. Said they were trespassing and I'd call the police. It worked."

"Can't they get on the land anywhere else?" Tim asked.

"I've got my own stockade," said Mr Andrews. "Not as posh as the one you're building: it's made of anything I could lay my hands on and that was mainly tin sheeting. Unsightly, but it's solid." He grinned like a wolf in the darkness. "No one will get on my land now. They won't make it like they made it outside. They've ruined the world, but not *my* world." Looking at him, Tim realized that Mr Andrews was not only a little more barmy than he had first imagined, but that he would be a very dangerous man to cross.

Through the thicket they could see a high grass bank which was bare earth lower down and had several large holes in it. They settled down behind the trees and Tim did as Mr Andrews had instructed: he swallowed himself, trying to imagine that he was

43

inside looking out. He soon got the trick of it and found his body no more than a protective layer that could be utterly still. He didn't feel any cramp or any desire to sneeze or make any sound whatever. He was utterly calm and at peace with himself. At a time in his life when everything seemed to have fallen apart, and after some very off-putting first encounters with the Howards, he had been accepted and now, as a member of Green Watch, was waiting for badgers to appear. His first adventure in the animal world.

Suddenly a dark form appeared out of the sett, and then another and another and another: four cubs, gambolling in the rough grass below the hole, rolling about, making little whiffling sounds and exuding a strange, rank smell. Soon some adults followed and proceeded to root about in the bushes. Then one of them detached itself from the group and headed off in the direction of the railway track.

"Hunting," indicated Mr Andrews in exaggerated mime. "Gone hunting."

For a few more seconds the other two badgers watched the cubs cavorting about. Then the idyll was shattered as a single shot cracked out, and then another. Something hit the side of the sett and the badgers froze. Two more shots followed and they froze again – as did Tim and Flower. They gazed at the badgers in horror. They seemed to be unhurt. But turning to Mr Andrews they saw he had uncoiled himself as if on a spring, and as the badgers dashed for the security of the sett, he launched himself forward with a wild and ragged cry. As he plunged towards some bushes Tim noticed the hunting badger return and also vanish down the hole. He looked ahead and saw Mr Andrews' leaping, enraged figure ploughing through the undergrowth like a huge tank.

Tim turned to Flower. "What do we do?" he asked.

"Follow him," she said, jumping up and heading towards the trail of flattened bushes. "He could kill someone."

But Mr Andrews seemed to have lost his quarry. When they caught up with him he was standing in a small clearing looking around him, almost sniffing the air in his fury.

"We'll split up," said Flower.

"No. He's armed," spat out Mr Andrews. "The swine's armed."

"He's not now," she replied.

"What?"

"Look!"

Tim and Mr Andrews followed her pointing finger to see an old shotgun lying on one of the paths. Mr Andrews stepped over and picked it up with a growl, then raced off down the path. Tim was about to follow when Flower grabbed his arm and said, "Hang on."

"Why?"

"It's a false trail."

"How do you know?"

"It's too neat. Look over there –" A few glades in

45

the other direction, outlined against the skyline, they could see the spectral shape of an oak tree, long since struck by lightning and denuded of foliage. Although dead, it was still a substantial size. "We'll start off this way, look as if we're following Mr Andrews, then we'll double back."

"Where to?"

"Keep walking. Like I told you."

They moved on purposefully.

"That oak's hollow. I think there's someone in there. Let Mr Andrews charge about, but we'll split up, either side of this path, and double back to the oak tree. Can you track?"

"Er –"

"Well, just move quietly then."

"One question: what do we do when we get to the oak tree?"

She looked at him impatiently. "What do you want to do? Brew up a cup of cocoa? We jump him of course."

"Supposing he's –"

"There're *two* of us, aren't there?" she snapped.

"That's right."

"So what's the problem?"

"No problem," agreed Tim hurriedly.

Once separated, Tim felt there was a *big* problem. He struggled doggedly through the dense undergrowth in the direction of the hollow oak, but Mr Andrews' wood seemed thicker and lusher than any he had been in before, and there was more underfoot to make a noise. A cloud of strong scent from invisible wild flowers and herbs hung over the woodland and the trees were barred with silvery moonlight. Tim, feeling almost unreal, moved as quietly as he could and wondered if he was keeping pace with Flower as they slowly advanced on their quarry.

Eventually, he was within metres of the tree. Every muscle and nerve in his body was tensing with effort. Straining his ears, he could catch no sound whatever, and certainly there was no sign of Flower. What was he to do? Go on? Stand still? Tim was in an agony of indecision. Then he thought he saw a movement: it was very slight but he was sure he had seen it. There was another movement, followed by a long silence. And then a sudden rush.

"Stay there." It was Flower's voice. He sprinted towards it, tripped, fell down and was on his feet again in seconds.

"Don't move," she was saying. "Just don't move."

A figure – tall, thin, scarecrow-like in the dark – detached itself from the tree and ran headlong towards Tim.

"Stop him," said Flower commandingly. "Just stop him."

The dark shadowy figure didn't seem to have seen him and ran on. At the last moment it veered away and instinctively Tim launched himself at it in a rugby tackle. They went down, Tim on top, and then Flower was on top of him. Somehow they spread themselves over the angular body, which thrashed, kicked and then, surprisingly, offered no resistance.

Between them they turned it over and pale moonlight caught features that were all too familiar.

"Luke!" gasped Flower. "What are you doing?"

"Get off."

"What are you *doing*?"

"Minding me own business. Taking a walk."

"You were tired – going to bed," said Flower.

"Changed me mind, didn't I?"

"You tried to kill the badgers, didn't you?"

"Dunno what you mean. Get *off*!"

"No. Tim, stay where you are."

Tim, who was holding down Luke's legs while Flower sat on his chest, silently nodded.

"It was you, wasn't it?"

"No."

From somewhere in the woodland came a bullish yell. Mr Andrews was still searching and he was quite close. It seemed his rage had not evaporated.

"You know what'll happen if he gets you, don't you?"

"Mr Andrews?"

"He's half barmy. In a terrible rage."

Another yell bellowed forth.

"Can't you hear him? Can't you imagine what he'll *do* to you?"

He nodded.

"Why did you do it?"

"He told me to."

"Who?"

"Johnson. He paid me to try and kill the badgers."

"You've never used a gun in your life. *Have* you?"

"He showed me. Him and Ray Harris."

"Who's Harris?"

"He's his partner. In the caravan business. He said – they said – if I managed to kill a badger the old man would go off his nut. Do something crazy – and then they'd have to take him off. For the public's protection, like."

"You idiot," said Flower. "Don't you realize he could have harmed you?"

"I'd got no money. It was worth the risk."

"How much did they pay you?"

"Fifty pounds."

"That all? For that sort of work."

"I gotta live."

"You prat. You going to tell?"

"On them? I daren't."

"You must. Tell the police. We could find you a job."

Luke turned his head away. "Yeah?" he said cynically.

"I mean it. We can *help* you."

"If I grass?"

"If you grass."

"No way."

Suddenly they could all hear the crashing of footsteps through the undergrowth.

"It's Mr Andrews," hissed Tim.

"He'll go potty when he knows it's Luke," said Flower quietly.

The thought of Mr Andrews' pottiness suddenly struck Luke very forcibly. "All right," he said.

"What do you mean, all right?"

"I mean, I'll grass."

Mr Andrews stood over them, breathing wheezily and looking baleful.

"You got him?"

"Yes," said Flower.

"Let me at him."

"No."

"What?"

"It's Luke."

"What's he doing?"

"Johnson paid him – to shoot the badgers – and get you so worked up that you might do someone an injury."

"I *will* do someone an injury." He knelt down by Luke. "What do you mean by it?"

"I got trouble at home."

"I know that."

"He paid me –"

"To shoot my badgers. I'll kill you."

"That's what I said," yelled Luke. "He's going to get me."

"No," said Flower. "No, he's not."

Mr Andrews did not kill Luke. But he frogmarched him back to the caravan, followed by Tim and Flower. Tim felt utterly exhausted now that the action was over.

Once in the caravan, Mr Andrews brewed more tea. He even made a cup very grudgingly for Luke.

"I'm going to turn you in," said Mr Andrews. "And you're going to tell the police what happened."

"They may not believe me," protested Luke.

"You'd better convince them. I want Johnson done. And who's this partner of his? Harris? The caravan king?"

"They was both there."

"Right. Finish that cup of tea and I'll take you right down to the police station." He turned apologetically to Flower. "You've done a great job, my darling, and you, Tim. Maybe my troubles are over."

"I wouldn't be too optimistic," said Flower.

He nodded and turned back to Luke. "You're not going to let me down, are you, Luke?"

"No, Mr Andrews," said Luke meekly.

"You're going to tell the police exactly what happened between you and Johnson and Harris, aren't you?"

"I'll try."

"And you'll succeed." He went over to the phone. "I'm going to ring your father, Flower. He'll meet us down there."

Mr Andrews marched Luke into the police station with the shotgun carried in an old blanket. Seb, looking worried, was there to meet them. He rushed up to Flower and Tim. "I should never have left you there."

Brian looked up from his book in the waiting-room. "Bit of excitement?" he asked.

Five minutes later Mr Andrews, prodding at the miserable Luke, was loudly telling his story to the sergeant and shortly afterwards Luke was put in one room with a CID officer and Mr Andrews, Flower and Tim were put in another while Seb and Brian waited uneasily outside. Once Flower and Tim had made and signed their statements they also came out.

"Well?" asked Seb. "Is this going to crack it?"

Tim shook his head. "It's only Luke's word for it. Suppose he does deny it? And Mr Andrews isn't coming across very well."

"What do you mean?" asked Seb sharply.

"He means he's gone all peculiar: says everyone's against him and that he's going to declare Independence."

"What?"

"He says he's going to call the land Badger Haven, and no one's coming in."

"What did the police say?" Seb asked.

"They said they'd heard the land might be compulsorily purchased by the council. That was the last straw. He's raving."

"They should never have told him that. There's never been anything positive said about that: it's just rumour. Speculation." Seb got abruptly to his feet. "I'll have to speak to them."

"It could make it worse, Dad," said Brian.

Seb sat down again and they waited in silence for another frustrating thirty minutes. Then a young CID man came in. He looked somewhat battered.

"I'd like a word," he said. "Unofficially."

Chapter Four

"I've been talking to young Luke," he said as he sat down. "By the way, my name's Henry Staff. I'm an Inspector in the CID."

Seb nodded impatiently.

"Trouble is, Luke Watson's story is rather – different from Mr Andrews. In fact they don't tie up at all."

"How's that?" asked Seb surprised. "It all seemed perfectly clear to us. Luke alleges that Johnson – or maybe Johnson and Harris – were responsible for paying him to –"

Inspector Staff interrupted gently. "He's not actually saying any of that. Watson's saying something different."

"What's that?"

"Watson alleges that he's never met Johnson or Harris."

"But he *told* me –" began Flower.

"And that he never touched the shotgun, or shot at any badgers on Mr Andrews' land."

"But you've got the shotgun –" began Seb impatiently.

"It's wiped clean of prints."

"Damn," said Flower angrily.

Tim didn't know what to think. Events kept changing all the time and he felt his mind could no longer keep pace with them. Besides, he was so desperately tired.

"But that's not all. Watson states that he's slept many times on Mr Andrews' property."

"In the engineers' office. He lets –" began Seb.

"Young runaways sleep there. We wish he wouldn't let them," said Staff grimly. "But he's made other allegations. He says that in a room off the engine shed Andrews has built up a cache of offensive weapons."

"*What?*"

"Petrol bombs in fact."

"I just don't believe it," said Seb.

"I gather your own property was petrol-bombed last night."

"Yes, but it couldn't have been anything to do with Mr Andrews."

"Why not?"

"We're his friends."

"Yes," Staff nodded gently. "He seems to have a grudge – a thing against this local farmer, Johnson.

Harris is presumably his partner. Well, grudge is understating it. Should I say obsession? He's brought some remarkable allegations against them."

"Such as?"

"I'm not at liberty to reveal them."

"I see. I still don't understand why Watson should tell you Mr Andrews has petrol bombs in his engine shed. It's patently ridiculous, and can easily be disproved."

"Now, I gather that an accident occurred to one of his locomotives – that it ran away and hit an aviary."

"Yes. That's correct. It happened this afternoon."

"Mr Andrews is claiming Mr Johnson took the brake off."

"I see. Well, obviously he believes he did."

"I hesitate to pay Mr Johnson a visit. Yet."

"Why?" Seb sounded belligerent.

"I shall be asking Mr Andrews to accompany us to his engine shed first."

"There'll be nothing there."

"Perhaps not."

"Can I go with you?"

"If Mr Andrews agrees."

"I think you'll find that he will."

"Do you have any reason to believe, Mr Howard, that Mr Andrews is – that the balance of his mind is –"

"He's eccentric. That's all. Are you trying to tell me that you think it was Mr Andrews who fire-bombed the windmill?"

"I'm not trying to –"

"Because if so, I can assure you you're wrong."

"You don't think he could have done it – perhaps to cast blame on Mr Johnson?"

"No," said Seb firmly. "I don't."

A police minibus took Mr Andrews, Seb, Flower, Brian and Tim, and a car carried the shifty-looking Luke, back to the railway yard. Certainly Mr Andrews' behaviour gave them some cause for concern. He seemed to have lost all his spirit and, ignoring everybody, sat hunched up, muttering and grumbling about Badger Haven, repeatedly telling himself that he would never leave his land again.

Seb leant over once or twice to comfort him, but the policeman sitting between them shook his head and Staff, sitting in front, said quietly, "I'd leave him alone if I were you, sir."

Once again they had arrived at the yard, Mr Andrews leapt out and, accompanied by two policemen, opened the gate. The disconnected siren did not wail and Mr Andrews paused, not seeming to understand what he should do next.

Inspector Staff then said, "Watson is going to join us. I would ask you not to speak to him or interfere with him in any way."

Seb nodded briefly, but Mr Andrews obviously didn't take in what Inspector Staff had said and when a sheepish Luke was brought up by another two policemen, he shook his head and said, "Luke, come to stay?"

Luke said nothing and Mr Andrews blinked

hesitantly. Inspector Staff went up to him and said gently, "Mr Andrews, we have reason to believe that you have something of interest to us in the engine shed. Will you show us in there?"

Looking like a lost and shambling giant, Mr Andrews nodded. Glancing across at Seb in bewilderment he said, "What do they want?" His voice shook.

"Just to take a look round, Alan. That's all."

"They won't take anything, or harm my engines?"

"No, Alan. They won't."

"And the badgers?"

"They'll be safe."

"I don't understand about young Luke. He doesn't sleep in the shed. He has his own quarters. I look after them, you know. All my young lads."

"We know you do, Mr Andrews," said Inspector Staff. "We won't keep you long."

"Shouldn't one of us be back at the windmill, Dad?" hissed Flower suddenly.

"No," said Brian with sudden force. "We're needed here, aren't we, Dad? Rusty will have to do his best."

Seb nodded very sadly and Flower took his hand.

"What's up?" hissed Tim.

"It's Mr Andrews," whispered Brian. "Something's gone wrong with him. He must have cracked up."

"This way."

Mr Andrews led the assorted group through one of the great big doors of the engine shed. Then he flicked a light switch and Tim gasped. It was absolutely amazing. They were met by a cathedral stillness and a reverential smell of oil and polish. The ceiling was lost in darkness; it was high and Tim could dimly see that it was vaulted. They were standing on a long thin pencil of a platform that led them past one highly polished locomotive after another. Mr Andrews led them on and, on the other side of the great space, separated by a turntable, were another two huge shining locomotives. They had different colours, different styles, but all four were like crouched, living beasts waiting to take off on a head of steam, to whistle and roar, to come to life in a cloud of smoking energy. Around them were dozens of polished brass lamps, levers, wheels, cogs, nuts, handles, gauges – and dozens of other engine parts whose functions Tim could not imagine. Screwed to the side of the shed were highly polished nameplates: Forester, Ironside, Sir Galahad, Peterloo, Iron Bridge, Head of Arkwright, Sir Roger de Coverley – dozens of them. And lining the sides of the platform were station signs: Walton-on-Thames, Tunbridge Wells, Etchingham, Stoke on Trent, Ambleside, Eccles, Dumpton Bottom and many others. It was incredible and Tim could hear the names chanting in his mind as Mr Andrews led them on.

Then he stopped and, in the eerie gloom of his railway palace, he spread out his arms and said, "Here we are. You are amongst friends. My friends. My engines. The Francis Drake, Pride of Wolverhampton, Light of the Isles, the Flying

Welshman. Only one old chum is missing." His voice broke. "The Queen Elizabeth. Bessie. She has been hurt."

"But is being rescued tomorrow," said Seb. "Don't worry, Alan. I've arranged for the crane to come tomorrow."

But Mr Andrews didn't seem to hear. He went over and patted the gleaming red bodywork of the Pride of Wolverhampton. "Don't worry, old friend. I'm here to protect you." He gave a funny kind of lurch and Seb put out a hand to steady him.

"Are you all right, Alan?"

He didn't reply. Then suddenly Mr Andrews began to recite:

"This is the night mail crossing the border
Bringing the cheque and postal order,
Letters for the rich, letters for the poor,
The shop at the corner and the girl next door."

Inspector Staff cleared his throat and one of the policemen moved a little closer to Mr Andrews. But he seemed oblivious.

"It was an age of steam," he said. "You know W. H. Auden?"

'Yes, Alan," said Seb quietly. "I know that poem. It's wonderful."

"It is indeed." Mr Andrews turned an excited, contorted face to them. His eyes flickered with a kind of inner fire. "Those badgers – they've seen the steam giants. They've prowled the fields by the line,

59

watching them roar past. They've sat and gazed in wonderment." He continued to recite, beating out the rhythm on a wooden bench with a spanner. Meanwhile, Tim noticed one of the policemen dodged through an arch leading off the main engine shed as Mr Andrews went on:

"Pulling up Beattock, a steady climb –
The gradient's against her but she's on time.
Past cotton grass and moorland boulder,
Shovelling white steam over her shoulder,
Snorting noisily as she passes
Silent miles of wind-bent grasses."

Mr Andrews stopped abruptly and said more quietly, "And in those wind-bent grasses, badgers, watching the great beasts snort their way along the tracks. Badgers. Unafraid."

The policeman came out of the arch. "Sir –"

Inspector Staff turned to him. "Yes?"

"I think I've found what we want."

"Just a minute." He went to join him and Mr Andrews turned with a sudden helplessness to Seb. "What are they doing?"

"Just having a look."

"They won't harm us?"

"No."

"Nor the badgers?"

"They're safe too, Alan." Seb went up and took his hand, pressing the gnarled old giant of a palm. "They're quite safe now."

Mr Andrews hung his great shaggy leonine head.

"Birds turn their heads as she approaches,
Stare from the bushes at her blank-faced
coaches . . ."

Inspector Staff returned. "Mr Andrews, will you
come through here with me?"

Tim saw Luke's face. It was a picture of utter
misery.

"Come on, Alan," said Seb. "Let's see if we can
clear all this up."

Tiredness forgotten, Tim followed.

The room was large and freshly white-washed and
the door hung open.

"I had to force the lock, sir," said the policeman
and Inspector Staff nodded.

"You've damaged the door," said Mr Andrews as
he stumbled in on Seb's arm.

Tim gasped, Flower gave a startled cry and Brian
muttered, "Oh no."

In the middle of the room there was a big sign
propped up against a table. Crudely painted, it read:
REPEL BORDERS. There were others. THIS IS
BADGER HAVEN – KEEP OUT. MY WORLD –
KEEP OUT. The lettering seemed to grow larger
and larger on each sign. STAY OFF THIS LAND
OR BE SHOT. The floor was covered with packing
cases. One was open. It was full of bottles. Each was
open, its neck stuffed with screwed-up rag. An old

dresser was the only other piece of furniture in the room. Piled up on its battered shelves were two shotguns, boxes of ammunition and longer boxes which read ELECTRICAL WIRE. On the floor in a corner were dozens of short posts.

"Well, Mr Andrews," said Inspector Staff. "What's all this?"

"My defences."

"When did you plan to use all these?"

"Against Johnson and Harris. The enemy."

"How can you be so sure they're your enemies?"

"They want to take it all away." Mr Andrews' voice rose to a faint wail. All the rage and anger in him seemed to have disappeared. His wail made Tim's stomach turn over and he felt a spreading chill of fear.

"Take it easy, Alan," said Seb.

"I'm afraid I shall have to arrest you, Mr Andrews. I'm charging you with the illegal –" But he never finished as Mr Andrews, like a felled oak, keeled over on to the floor. Seb broke his fall as he went down.

"Alan, Alan." He bent over him, feeling for his pulse. Then grey-faced, he looked up at Inspector Staff. "Radio for an ambulance," he snapped. "Fast."

Tim was so exhausted that he slept dreamlessly until lunchtime the next day. When he woke, at first he had no idea where he was and when he remembered he couldn't immediately recall the events of last night. When he did, they came back to him in a muddled blur as he saw himself being half-carried, half-helped up the stairs to bed with Rusty in barking, dancing attendance. He remembered Seb putting him into bed – but no more.

The sun was streaming through his window as Tim got stiffly out of bed and looked out into the garden. Below him, the fencing barricade was already half in place and he could see Flower and Brian dragging more across. He pulled down the window. The air was fresh. Why were they still making the barricade, he wondered. There seemed some reason against it. Then he remembered Mr Andrews' engine shed.

"Hi."

Flower stopped. "Hallo, lazybones."

"We've been working since six," said Brian. But he was grinning.

"Rubbish," said Flower. "You've only just got up."

"How's Mr Andrews?"

"I've been to see him. Dad's still with him. He's not good. Had a coronary."

Tim felt conscience-stricken. "I shouldn't have been up here asleep," he groaned.

"Rubbish," said Brian unexpectedly. "You deserve all the sleep you can get."

Tim wondered why he had ever thought them so remote, so perfect. He was one of them now. Thank God. "Is Mr Andrews going to live?"

"Yes, but he'll be in hospital for weeks."

"What about the yard?"

"The police are there."

"Is he going to be arrested?"

"We don't know. But Dad's sure he didn't do it to us – would never do it to us."

Tim felt reassured. He had been so confused. It really had looked as if Mr Andrews had gone mad. "What do we do now, then?" he asked.

"Clear his name," said Flower. "That's what Dad thinks we should do. Clear his name, protect his land and –"

"And protect ours too," put in Brian.

"Make yourself some breakfast," said Flower. She looked at her watch. "And there's a Green Watch meeting at two, when Dad gets back from the hospital." She looked up at him and Tim saw anxiety in her face. "Whatever we do must be quick," she said.

"Johnson? The police?"

"Mr Andrews. If he knows we've cleared him and saved his land, he'll recover. If not . . ." She broke off and looked away.

"We're going to have to move fast."

Seb sat at the Green Watch Round Table, set in the centre of the cabin-like main room. Tim hadn't noticed it particularly before, for it had been covered with an untidy jumble of papers and books. But now it had been swept clear, he saw it was made of very lightly polished oak and inlaid into it was a detailed map of the world, hand drawn and beautifully coloured.

"It was done by an old fisherman," Seb had told him as they cleared up the room together. "It's the

64

Green Watch Round Table; anyone who sits round it has an equal say with everyone else." Now Seb was at his most coldly purposeful, just as he had been a few days ago when Tim had been frozen on the rocks. But the big difference was Tim knew him now, and was beginning to understand him.

"If we don't move fast," he said, "the old boy will peg out on us."

"But what can we do?" For once Flower sounded despondent and Brian didn't look much better, but Tim could already sense how strong Seb was in a crisis.

"I've told him we're doing a lot – and I'm pretty sure he understood me. For instance, we need to get on and search that farm – see if Johnson's got any more Molotov cocktails around."

"You think he planted them on Mr Andrews?" asked Tim quietly.

"I'm sure he did."

"But why didn't he *say* so?" said Flower. "He just stood there – and it looked as if he'd made them all."

"By that stage he was so confused he didn't know *what* he was saying – and he is getting more and more ill by the minute. So if we can only get in and search Johnson's farm, find something – anything – incriminating, then he'll have some hope."

"Would they be fool enough to leave anything around?" asked Brian.

"They wouldn't expect us to invade them." Seb seemed very sure of what he was saying.

"Let's get this right, Dad." Flower spoke slowly. "Are you saying we're going to break in?"

"We're going to have a look round."

"At night?"

"Yes."

"Inside?"

"If we have to."

"That means we *are* going to break in."

"Yes," agreed Seb. He looked across at Tim. "You don't have to join us. I mean, you probably shouldn't." But Tim couldn't bear his sudden uncharacteristic hesitation.

"I'm coming," he said. "Try and stop me."

Seb grinned. "We don't often break the law," he said.

"When *do* you break the law?" enquired Tim.

"Well, we've broken a few maritime laws, haven't we, Brian? Remember when we sailed *Windspit* into the nuclear zone? And when that frigate almost rammed us in the South Pacific?"

Brian and Flower nodded, smiling. What amazing adventures they had, thought Tim, wondering if he would ever be included in the more exotic ones.

"But apart from this rather dodgy little enterprise," said Seb, returning to the present problem, "we're going to have to move into the rail yard – at least some of us will."

Flower nodded. "Suppose Tim and I stay at the house and carry on with the stockade while you and Brian move into Mr Andrews' caravan. Have we still got those walkie-talkies?"

"Yes," Seb looked approving. "I'll dig them out."

Tim, meanwhile, was overjoyed. Flower was actually considering him part of the team, actually suggesting they stayed together. It was incredible. "Rusty will help us," he said proudly, hoping that Rusty wouldn't go and do something to let him down. Like going to sleep on the job for instance.

"OK," said Seb. "I'll check out the farm."

"You won't," said Flower. "We'll help on that one."

"Then we'll have to draw their fire," replied Seb thoughtfully.

"How?" asked Brian doubtfully.

"I'll ring him. Now." Seb lifted the phone and dialled. When he spoke, he sounded different. Very different.

"Señor Johnson?" Seb switched on the amplifier so the rest of Green Watch could hear Johnson's voice, which was both rude and puzzled.

"What?"

"It is Carlos Fuentes here."

"Who?"

"I am a scout for the Spanish hypermarket chain Coroba."

"Never heard of them."

"We are looking for a large site in this area."

"What for?"

"To open a new hypermarket." Seb raised his eyes to heaven at Johnson's slowness. "I'm told you have a large site . . ."

"A large site?" A note of interest suddenly entered

Johnson's voice. "I own a very large site."

"But I believe – my contacts tell me – you are in dispute with a Mr Andrews –"

"He's sitting on my land, and I can't get the law enforced. But it shouldn't be long before I'm in possession."

"I believe you plan a caravan site on this area?"

"Yes. Or part of it."

"We would not want the whole site." Seb's Spanish accent never slipped. "Perhaps we could discuss . . ."

"How do I know you're genuine?" said Johnson warily.

"I have documents to prove it. And if you are able to prove the land is yours, then I should be interested in making you an offer."

An excited note of greed entered Johnson's voice and Tim knew, with a growing sense of elation, that he had fallen for Seb's trick. But would he be able to keep it up?

"I'm definitely interested, but it's taking me a long time to prove . . ."

"We would be able to bring our own lawyers in. They could be helpful to you. They are knowledgeable in such matters."

"Are they now?"

"However, I am here for a limited time only, and I would like to explain my plans in more detail."

"Couldn't we meet?"

"Perhaps. I am staying at the Riverside Country Club. You know where that is?"

"Just outside Canterbury. On the Ashford Road?"

"Yes. I have a dinner engagement tonight and fly back to Spain early tomorrow, but I could meet you in the bar at, say, ten-thirty. Would that be convenient?"

"Well, it's a bit late, but, yes, I can manage it. How do I recognize you?"

Seb laughed. "I am afraid I am a very large man with a dark complexion. Sadly, I am completely bald. You can't miss me, Mr Johnson."

"Doesn't sound like it. I'll be there."

"I shall look forward to meeting you. Ten-thirty in the bar then." Seb put the phone down and his three companions burst out laughing.

"You were great, Dad," said Brian.

"You went a bit over the top at the end," warned Flower.

"Mmm. Swarthy and bald. What do you reckon, Tim?" asked Seb.

"I reckon you were dead convincing," said Tim loyally.

Chapter Five

"It's time," said Seb, looking at his watch. Tim shivered. What had seemed like a great adventure earlier in the day now felt very off-putting. It was dark, a high wind was blowing and it was gusting with rain.

"How long have we got?" said Brian.

Seb looked at his watch again. "He leaves, say, in ten minutes. Takes him an hour to get there and maybe twenty minutes hanging round and accosting people. Then he gives up and comes home. We've got two and a half hours at the outside."

Rusty barked accusingly as they left in the landrover. Five minutes later, Seb drew into a lay-by.

"From here on it's overland – and on foot."

"Ssh. Not a sound."

"Is that the farm?" hissed Tim.

"It's over there. And there he goes."

The large dark shape of a van shot out of the yard and up the track.

"Does he live alone?"

"Yes, his wife walked out on him last year."

"No children?"

"No children." Seb put a strong, cool hand on Tim's. "Stop worrying. I've checked it all out. We'll stay here for another five minutes. And then move in. Flower and Brian, you take the outhouses. Tim and I will move in on the house. You two get back here in half an hour and keep guard. OK?"

They all muttered that it was.

The house was a mass of dark shadows.

"He doesn't even keep a dog," whispered Seb. "Not an animal lover, our Mr Johnson."

They were at the back and Seb was trying a window. "Got it," he whispered triumphantly.

"Shall I crawl through?" asked Tim. "Then I can open the door."

"Wear these."

"Gloves?"

"We don't want to leave any marks behind."

Feeling like a real crook. Tim clambered in at the window and on to what he soon discovered was the evil-smelling draining board of the kitchen sink. From there, he jumped lightly down to the floor and hurried towards the back door. He scrabbled with the

71

large key, it clicked, he turned the handle and the door was open. It was all very easy but Tim couldn't stop trembling.

"You OK?" asked Seb as he crept in.

"I keep shaking."

"So you should. It'll keep you on your toes."

"Where're we going?"

"Start at the top and work our way down."

The farmhouse was small and ill cared for. There were no attics, simply a sad and squalid bedroom with an empty room next to it. Tim and Seb searched both but didn't find anything. They crept back downstairs and were just about to search the big kitchen, when headlights swept the yard.

Seb grabbed Tim and they both hit the floor at the same time.

"He's back," hissed Tim.

"I can't think why." Seb's voice was muffled. "I just can't think why."

The van pulled up and the lights were switched off. They froze, hugging the cold lino. Tim prayed that Flower and Brian had heard the van too and hidden. He sensed that Seb was thinking exactly the same thing.

Footsteps resounded across the hard surface of the yard and a cow lowed disconsolately. No dogs, thank God we knew he had no dogs, thought Tim. A key turned in the lock. Seb was desperately looking round for somewhere to hide. Suddenly he grabbed Tim's shoulder and they both shot to their feet, heading for the half-open pantry door. They were only just inside when the kitchen was flooded with light.

The pantry door was ill fitting and through the crack between hinges and wall, Tim could see a tall, thin-shouldered man in a sports jacket and rather grubby-looking dark trousers. He was clean shaven with sandy, thinning hair. He went to the telephone and dialled. It rang for a long time before it was answered.

"Where the hell have you been? Eh? No, I forgot to ring you earlier. In fact I came back. From where? Oh, just a business meeting. Yes, a business meeting at this time of night. Now, make it snappy or I'm going to be late. Call box? I didn't have your number. I can never remember it. No, I'm not cracking up, just got a lot on my plate. I remembered, didn't I? In the end I remembered. No. I don't know how the old boy is, but I don't think he's going to live and that's gonna make the job a damn sight easier. It was just that we should – you should – get rid of those badgers tonight. Yes, tonight. I been thinking in the car that once those bloody conservation people really get going we could have trouble. Other conservation groups. Holding things up. So if you pump enough gas down there tonight . . . How can I be with you? I've got a business meeting, I told you. And I'm getting later every minute. You get rid of those badgers, and if the old boy croaks, it's all going to make it easier in court. He'll probably have another heart attack if someone tells him the badgers have been done. Get up there about – I don't know – after midnight anyway. Take Luke with you. Unreliable? All the kids are; but we can tell Luke what to do, can't we? So you're all set up. Right? Get stuck in."

He put down the receiver and swore as he looked at his watch. Turning out the light he tore down the passage, banging the front door behind him. The van door slammed, the engine revved and he was off, turning with a screech of brakes and then roaring away down the lane.

"It's going to be a long night," said Seb as they emerged from the panty. "We're fighting on two fronts now."

"There's nothing out there," said Flower as she and Brian came in, looking fearful. "We hid."

"So did we," Seb replied and then he told them about Johnson's ominous telephone call. "So we'll have to move. It's just the downstairs now. It's too modern for a cellar."

All four began a methodical search of the living-room and kitchen. As they searched, however, they kept thinking of Mr Andrews' wilderness and the badgers. Seb looked repeatedly at his watch as they worked, obviously worried about what might be happening to them.

"What did he mean about it being easier if Mr Andrews died?" asked Brian.

"Well, of course it'd probably be a piece of cake for him then," said Seb impatiently. "But Alan's not going to die, so it doesn't apply."

"Seb." Tim suddenly had an unpleasant thought. "If there weren't any buildings – if everything was flattened – wouldn't it be easier for Johnson to get the land?"

"Probably. Poor old Alan would have to sell the land to him at a knock-down price then. Settle out of court."

"So mightn't he try and burn it all down?"

"He might. That's why Mr Andrews kept guard up there. And that's why we should be there. So let's keep looking."

They searched more intensively for the next twenty minutes, making sure they left everything as undisturbed as possible. Then Brian said, "Hang on."

They went back into the gloomy kitchen again.

"What's up?" Seb glanced at him keenly.

"This floor sounds hollow. It's a different sound. Under the mat."

Flower and Tim yanked it up. Beneath it were boards rather than a concrete base.

"There's a slight groove in one of these," said Seb. He applied his fingers, pulled and the board sprang up. "There's something here. Where's the torch?"

Flower passed it to him and then gasped as the beam illuminated the dark space underneath. Neatly packed into it was a rifle, a packet of cartridges and a number of bottles with rags stuffed into them. They were identical to the ones in Mr Andrews' storeroom.

"Will this prove anything?" asked Brian.

"It might," Seb replied. "And I bet he hasn't got a licence for this gun. Hang on, there's something else." He dug around and lifted out a grey envelope.

It was addressed to Mr Johnson.

"What's in it?" demanded Flower.

"Wait while I get it open, it's not stuck down." Seb scrabbled at the envelope and eventually pulled from it a buff document. He spread it out, reading it while Brian continued to hold the torch.

"Good God!"

"What is it?" Flower was beside herself with curiosity, as were Tim and Brian.

"It's a land deed."

"What's that?"

"A map. It must have been drawn up after Johnson sold the land to Sampson. It shows all Johnson's farm, but the railway site isn't on it." Seb felt in the envelope again. "And look at this!" he added. "What a find. This is the land deed for the railway site. In other words, the two of them are just what we want. Obviously Johnson stole this one, and hid the whole lot together. Point is I don't think Alan ever knew this existed, let alone that it was stolen. He would have told me. It must have been in that mound of filthy papers in his caravan. The two deeds just about prove everything."

Brian wasn't listening. He was staring at the door.

"What's up, Brian?"

"Thought I heard something. Maybe not."

Tim could feel the hairs on the back of his neck rising. He thought that only happened in stories. Now he knew it was for real. Surely Brian was mistaken. Brian *must* be mistaken.

"It's nothing."

A rush of relief filled Tim.

"What are you going to do with them, Dad?" asked Flower.

"I'm going to keep them." Seb put the documents in his inside pocket. Then the back door swung open.

Tim thought that his heart had stopped. The light flashed on and the kitchen was filled with hard strip lighting. The man was stocky and wore a business suit that failed to look smart and succeeded only in looking very flashy indeed. He smelt of cigars and expensive cars. In his hand was a gun. He spoke slowly and softly.

"When I see torchlight in a window I know the owner can't be at home." He smiled. "I'm putting you under citizen's arrest. You're nicked."

"That's fine," said Seb.

Why hadn't they heard a car, wondered Tim over and over again. He was soon to find out.

"And when I see a landrover abandoned down a side road, I say to myself, all can't be well. There must be some villains abroad. So I left my own vehicle, and took a little walk."

Seb stood up.

"Don't come any closer," said the man.

"I wouldn't want to."

"And those documents. Let's have them."

"No chance."

"Let's have them now."

"These prove something important about a friend

of mine and his property. So I've no intention of handing them over."

"Let's have them," the man said for the third time.

"No."

"You're breaking and entering."

"Needs must."

"I'll call the police."

"Go ahead."

Surely, thought Tim, if they *do* come, we're in real trouble. Whatever we've found.

The man hesitated and Seb laughed. "Called your bluff?"

"No." He levelled the gun at Flower. "But it's like this: you broke in. I apprehended you. There was a struggle and this gun went off. The little girl got hurt."

"They wouldn't wear that."

"No?"

"Do you have a licence for that gun?"

"Yes, I do." He was still levelling it at Flower.

"Put it down."

"No."

"You'll –" There was a slight edge to Seb's voice now.

Tim could hardly believe what was happening and Brian seemed dazed. The only calm person was Flower, gazing steadily back at the man with the gun.

"You know what," she said.

He ignored her.

"We've got someone else outside."

He smiled indulgently.

"Someone who's coming in now."

He continued to smile indulgently.

"The door's opening behind you." Flower's voice was still very level. "Quickly, you idiot, grab him." There was a sudden urgency in her tone. For a brief second the man in the flashy suit glanced behind him. It was enough. Brian launched himself at his pin-striped legs with a primeval yell.

He toppled over with Brian on top of him and the gun went off with a deafening report. But Seb was there too and the man kicked and swore as they pinned him down.

"Give it to me." Seb wrested the gun away.

"They're up there now," breathed the man with a grim satisfaction. "Gassing your badgers."

For a moment Seb relaxed his hold. The man twisted under him and sent him flying, the gun rattling on to the floor. With surprising agility for such a big man, he was on his feet in seconds, darting for the gun, snatching it up and grabbing Flower at the same time. He gave another grin of satisfaction whilst wheezing heavily.

Slowly Seb picked himself up. "I suppose you're Ray Harris?" he breathed.

"Let's just say I'm an interested party."

"Let her go."

"When I'm safely out – with the documents."

"No way."

"I'm not prepared to kill your daughter –"

"Of course you're not."

79

"But I *will* hurt her."

"Hurt her?" Seb's voice faltered.

"Don't listen to him, Dad." Amazingly, Flower seemed quite composed. But looking at her, Tim guessed that she didn't really believe what was happening to her.

"I'll hurt her. Give me those papers."

"No, Dad."

The man tightened his grip around Flower's neck and jammed the base of the gun against her cheek. She winced. "You don't have to fire these things to do damage," he wheezed.

"All right."

"Hand 'em over."

"No, Dad. Don't – please don't –"

"Take them and let her go."

"I'll push her towards you, and as she comes you give me the papers."

"OK."

"And remember, I've still got this." He lifted the gun.

"No, Dad –"

He pushed her hard and grabbed at the documents Seb was holding out. The exchange was made and Flower ran into her father's arms.

"You bastard!" Brian shouted.

"Don't abuse me, son. And stay exactly where you are. Don't try to follow me." He backed away towards the door, and then hurried through it. They heard him walking across the yard. Then he broke into a little shuffling run.

"Dad – you shouldn't –" Flower wept, her head buried against Seb's chest.

Tim saw that Seb was shaking, but he didn't know whether it was from relief or fury.

"You shouldn't have done it, Dad," repeated Flower.

"Done what?"

"Given him the documents."

But he was waving something in her face. "There were quite a few copies, you know. I gave them to him. Except these two."

Brian clapped his hands. "Dad, you're brilliant."

"I know," said Seb. He held Flower away from him. "I know I'm brilliant." He looked across at Tim and winked. But all three of them could see his hands were still shaking.

"Come on."

"The badgers?" asked Tim.

"They're in real danger. We'll have to go over there," said Seb.

"What about the mill?" asked Brian.

"We're going to have to leave that to Rusty," said Seb brusquely.

But what if they hurt him, wondered Tim with a stab of fear.

Chapter Six

Another late night, thought Tim. But he didn't feel in the least tired – just enormously elated that Green Watch had accepted him so whole-heartedly. His fear at the events of the night had been overlaid by his joy at being one of them, but now, when he thought about it, he began to realize the very real danger they were in. These men – Johnson and his friend – were obviously going to let nothing stand in the way of getting their hands on Mr Andrews' land.

As they drove towards the railway yard, Tim gave voice to a thought that had been nagging at him ever since they had got back into the landrover. "Seb?"

"Yeah?"

"If we can prove Mr Andrews owns the land – and we can – why don't we just go to the police? Won't they stop Johnson and co doing all this?"

"Nothing we can *prove* against them right now."

"But that man – and the gun he had – and the way he threatened Flower –"

"Sure. It's our word against his."

"So. There's four of us."

There was a short, uncomfortable silence, then Brian said quietly, "Truth is – Green Watch isn't – exactly popular with the authorities – and that includes the police."

"But why?"

"They think we're troublemakers," said Seb. "A bunch of weirdo troublemakers."

"And we are," said Flower with a giggle. "At least, that's the way we sometimes look. After all, we support causes that other people ignore – or won't take on – or stay away from."

Tim nodded. He understood. "But what are we going to do?"

"Catch them red-handed," said Seb.

"Isn't that going to be a bit tricky?"

Seb nodded. He pulled a camera out from the shelf under the dashboard. "This is quite sophisticated," he said. "If we can photograph them in action – perhaps even take them prisoner –"

Tim stared at him in amazement. "But if he owns the land, surely the police –" he began again.

Seb smiled patiently. "He may own it, but these guys are trying to prove that he's such a nuisance that all his affairs should be investigated. And so far they're doing pretty well: one locomotive in someone's garden, fire bombs and an armoury on the premises, a possible fire-bomb attack against us, trying to frame Johnson, etc. They're building up quite a case against him – and we have to smash that. Maybe tonight."

The copse was completely still. There was no wind at all and the night was warm and mellow. They waited for an hour. Surely, whoever was coming should have appeared by now. Harris had said they were there already. Their original relaxation when badger watching had given way to tension, and when the badgers eventually came out they snuffled the air cautiously, as if sensing the anxiety around them. They played for a while, two of them went hunting, the others returned to the sett, and nothing untoward happened at all.

Tim looked at his watch. It was almost three am. If anything was happening up at the engine shed it was unlikely that they would hear it: the copse was too far away.

"Maybe they're not coming after all," whispered Brian.

"We heard him on the telephone. Telling them to go tonight. They must be coming."

"Maybe our pin-striped friend tipped them off," said Seb thoughtfully. "Perhaps they think too much has happened too fast."

"What shall we do?" asked Tim, thinking suddenly how wonderful it would be to be in bed. He was also getting increasingly worried about Rusty. They shouldn't have left him on his own. He should never have agreed to it. Was he so overawed by Green Watch? So desperate to belong that he would even put his beloved Rusty at risk by not protesting? He felt a wave of self-loathing.

"We'll give it till dawn," said Seb. "Then I'll stay here and you lot can go back."

"We can't leave you here alone, Dad –" began Flower.

"You can, and you will. Hang on –"

"What's that?" Brian turned.

"You hear what I hear?"

"Someone – something moved. Up in the engine shed."

"There's loads of cats up there," said Flower, "but I don't think we could hear them from here."

"It didn't sound like a cat," insisted Brian.

Tim's heart plummeted. In his mind's eye he saw Rusty. Rusty lying dead. But of course Rusty wasn't here. He was back at the windmill.

"What shall we do?" asked Flower.

"Get up there." Seb was already on his feet.

"We can't *all* go," she said. "I'll stay here."

"I'll stay with you," said Tim.

"No." She was firm.

"Why not?"

"If there's trouble up there, you'll all be needed. And if there's trouble down here, I can run for you."

"Trouble?" said Seb. "I think we have it already. Look at that locomotive – the one that's half in and half out of the shed. It's moving. Very slowly. But it's moving.

Tim, Brian and Seb left Flower still crouching in the copse and ran for the engine. It was definitely moving down the gradient. And it was picking up speed.

"If it hits the other one – the one that's still in that garden – it could push it through the house."

"How do we stop it?" panted Tim.

"I know how to do it. We just need to catch up with it."

But as they ran towards it, the engine continued to gather speed.

"Stop it. We must stop it somehow, Dad," gasped Brian.

"It's really moving."

Tim was ahead, nearing the engine now. It looked enormous, like some dark ship of the night as it floated silently and swiftly along the rails. Grass rustled around it and a bat soared above its funnel as if urging it on.

"Go for it, Tim."

"I can't stop it –"

"Go for it. I'm with you."

Seb was a few paces behind now with Brian bringing up the rear.

"*Go* for it."

And Tim was beside the rolling monster, looking for a projection to hang on to – and finding it. He grabbed the footplate handle, yelled out for he thought he would fall, and somehow dragged himself on board. It was terrifying; directly he got his bearings, Tim could feel the cold metal, the silent speed, the terrible feeling of being out of control.

"Seb!" he screamed in desperation. For a moment he couldn't see him. He wasn't there! "Seb!"

Then he saw his strong brown hand on the handle and Tim grabbed at Seb's sweater as he hauled himself up.

"Watch out, that's real Shetland wool," he said, trying to detach himself from Tim's clutching hands. Then he was in the centre of the footplate, grabbing, pulling, almost bending a huge lever. "Let's hope she stops in time," he muttered.

But she showed no sign of stopping, despite the screaming of brakes.

"Look," yelled Tim. "I can see the other engine."

Sure enough, further down the gradient they could see the rear of the other locomotive stuck out at a crazy angle. And they were silently nearing it at a really amazing speed.

"Are there any other brakes?" yelled Tim.

"No," said Seb grimly. "I've done all I can. I think she's slowing."

"Is she?"

"But just in case, brace yourself."

The rear of the other engine seemed to be getting nearer at a very alarming rate, but they were slowing, and sparks from the locked wheels were flashing up

high over the countryside. With agonizing unpre-
dictability the engine ground to a halt – metres
behind the first one.

Tim groaned. "Suppose they send out another?"
he said.

Seb looked at him in horror.

"They might," Tim insisted. "It's all downhill."

Without saying anything Seb leapt off the engine
and started to run back to the shed. As he did so,
another engine began to emerge from the doors and
to travel down the gradient towards them.

"Whoever it is," yelled Seb, "they're setting them off
one by one."

"I'll get in there," said Brian.

"You won't. But do you remember how to stop
'em?"

"Yes."

"Run like hell. She's only going slowly now."

Brian did as he was told while Seb dashed on,
heading for the engine shed.

There were two engines left, and one was on the
turntable. It was easy to set them loose, he thought.
Mr Andrews had been wrong about that. All anyone
had to do was to unblock the wheels, for the engine
shed itself was on a very slight gradient. Seb ran up to
the engine on the turntable, but there was no one
around, and when he checked the last remaining
locomotive, there was no one there either. He stood
very still, listening, but he couldn't hear a sound.

The second engine that had left the shed that morning clanked to a halt about fifty yards from the one that Tim was still on. They were silhouetted in the dark now: one half in and half out of the garden and the other two silently purposeful, stark against the skyline that was just beginning to show the first pale flush of dawn.

"What's he doing?" yelled Tim.

"Searching the engine shed," shouted back Brian. Then he said, "Don't make so much noise."

Tim waited in the cab of his engine, staring out at the grey copse straight in front of him. He could see no sign of Flower, but as he looked he caught a sudden, fleeting movement. Someone broke cover and ran towards the sett. They were carrying something heavy. Another shadowy figure followed.

"Brian," Tim hissed. "Brian." But his voice didn't carry and he didn't dare to call again. Oh God, thought Tim, they're going to gas them. They're going to gas the badgers now. And it's as if they're playing with us: sending engines down the gradient while they gas the very animals we've come to save. Green Watch was fully stretched – over-stretched. And where was Flower? And what was happening to Rusty?

But despite all these confusing thoughts, Tim had only one instinct: to run towards the badgers, to protect them. And with this in mind he jumped off the footplate and ran towards the copse. For a few seconds Brian watched him. Then he followed.

There was no one there. Seb had combed the engine shed twice now, checking every nook and cranny, including the inspection pits and the various workshops and bays that led off the main shed. There was no sign of anyone. He turned away and hurried back outside, but when he checked the sentinel engines there was no sign of either Brian or Tim. He glanced anxiously towards the copse. It was then that he heard a shrill cry of pain. It sounded like Flower's voice and Seb began running in the direction of the copse. Then he heard another sound: that of a car, a car moving very fast.

"Stop!"

The two men turned and Tim saw they weren't men but boys – and one of them was Luke. The other was shorter, stockier, and was wearing motorcycle gear.

"What the hell do you want?" Luke scoffed.

"You have to stop."

"Why?"

"You can't *do* that!" Tim's voice was hoarse.

"They're a nuisance, them badgers," said the stocky boy. "We got instructions." He sounded confident and self-important.

"Who from?"

"The owner."

"Mr Andrews?"

"The owner," the boy repeated doggedly. He looked across at the locomotives. "What's happening with them engines?"

"Happening?" Brian joined them. He looked very angry. "Some idiot let them loose."

Luke laughed. "You're having quite a night of it, aren't you?"

"And what have you done with my sister?"

"Sister. I didn't see no sister."

"Where is she?"

"I said, I didn't see no sister."

Brian sprang at the motorcycle boy, who backed off at first, then suddenly lunged forward and hit Brian hard on the side of the head. He staggered back and then fell to the ground. Tim didn't know what to do; he knew he wouldn't stand a chance against them but he had to do something for Brian, who was lying on the ground, groaning.

"You shouldn't have done that," he said inadequately.

"And he shouldn't have interfered," snapped Luke.

Tim went over to Brian and tried to help him up, but Brian fell back, pulling Tim with him, and they both went sprawling, leaving Luke and his companion to laugh uproariously. Then they stopped laughing and when Tim looked up he saw Seb standing there.

"What the hell are you two doing?" he said sharply.

"Er –"

"And what have you done to my son?"

"He attacked –"

"And where's my daughter?"

"I don't know who your daughter is."

91

"No?" Seb stepped forward and grabbed the motorbike boy's arm, savagely twisting it up behind his back. "Where is she?"

"Don't you –"

"Where is she?"

"You're hurting me."

"Where is she?"

"You leave him alone," said Luke.

"And you shut up," replied Tim, eagerly backing Seb up.

"Where is she?" repeated Seb.

"All right, I'll tell you."

"Where?"

"Let go."

"You going to tell me?"

"Yes." Seb let him go and the boy rubbed his arm. "She went with the bloke."

"*What*?"

"The bloke. Big bloke. In his car."

"Who is he?"

"Friend of Johnson's."

"Harris?"

"Yeah," said Luke sullenly.

Seb's face was white and strained in the dawn light.

"I'm going after him," he said. "But first – you two – if you don't clear off with all your equipment I'll thump the living daylights out of you." He turned to Luke. "You ought to be ashamed of yourself – after all Mr Andrews has done for you."

"I need the money," said Luke simply.

Suppose they don't go, or go and then come back,

wondered Tim. But he could see Seb was thinking the same thing.

"On second thoughts, you two'd better come with me," he said.

"S'pose they jump you, Dad?"

"They won't." Seb was very confident. "I've got some rope in the back. I'm going to tie them together."

"We're not going anywhere," said the motorbike boy, but when Seb went up to him he quickly changed his mind. "All right," he said. "We're coming."

"You stay here, you two. There's absolutely no one in the engine shed now, so I'm going to get Flower." His voice shook and Tim glanced at Brian. She could be miles away by now. So how could he hope to find her? And what would Harris do with her?

"What now?"

"We'd better stay here. In the copse. Unless we split up," said Brian.

"Let's stay together," replied Tim. "But maybe we'd better move around. I mean alternate between the engine shed and here."

"OK."

They began to walk hurriedly up towards the shed, casting backward glances at the copse and the sett. Both Brian and Tim felt horribly torn between the two parts of Mr Andrews' empire that they were trying to protect.

When they reached the huge engine shed, Brian

stood back and looked at it and the satellite collection of jumbled outbuildings that surrounded it. "Dad searched the whole place and found no one."

"That's what he said."

"I wonder –" He paused reflectively.

"Wonder what?" asked Tim impatiently. Brian could be exasperatingly slow sometimes.

"If there could be a hidden room or anything?"

"But surely –"

"You know what Mr Andrews is like. Full of peculiar secrets, special secrets of his own."

"You mean someone could be hiding in it?"

"Maybe. Let's go and look round inside. But first, I'll just memorize the layout." He took another look and then yawned.

"You tired?"

"Haven't thought – in all the excitement."

"Green Watch certainly keeps you on your toes," said Tim. "But it isn't half tiring."

They had searched everywhere, but Brian didn't seem satisfied. "Funny thing."

"What's that then?"

"Well, it doesn't add up." He went to a blank, greasy wall that was covered in oil stains. "It stops here, but when you're outside it sticks out." He tapped at the wall. "It doesn't *sound* hollow."

"Wait a minute." There was a pile of old boxes and empty plastic oil cans at the end, but Tim had noticed the floor around them had been swept. He began to pull them down, making enough noise to warn off any intruder. "Look."

"A steel shutter."

"And it looks new," said Tim. "It works on this crank. We've got one in the garage at home." He pulled and the shutter slid up, revealing a dark space behind. There was a peculiar smell: a mixture of oil and polish. He walked in. Brian followed, fumbling for a light switch. Eventually he found it.

"Wow." Tim stared ahead in amazement.

"Shut up, or I'll stuff gags in your mouths as well."

The landrover was hurtling along a twisting B road with Luke and his friend trussed up with thick ropes in the back. Occasionally they moaned and Luke had just said he felt sick.

"Where would he have taken her?" snapped Seb after a few minutes of grudging silence.

"How should we know?"

"You're telling me the truth, are you? Because if not –"

"I'm telling you the truth."

"I'm going to try the farm, and if I find you've lied . . ."

"Johnson's?"

"Where else?" He hurled the landrover down an even narrower lane and screeched to a halt in a lay-by. "I'm going to ram something in your mouths, lads. Just till I get back."

They protested but he gagged them and then left, locking the landrover carefully.

The room smelt of paint and they could see that it was a brightly lit spray shop. In it were two large and very beautiful vintage Rolls Bentleys. One was black and white, the other black. Both were gleaming with fresh paint and polish.

"Look at this," said Tim.

There was a small table by the door. On it were an electric kettle and a cup. The kettle was still warm.

Chapter Seven

The farmhouse was gaunt and skeletal in the early morning light. Without hesitation, Seb went straight up to the front door and thundered on it. The sound was sharp and hollow in the stillness. He kept on banging until the door finally opened and an unkempt Johnson stood on the threshold.

"What the hell – ?"

"Where's my daughter?"

"Eh?"

"Where is she?"

"I don't know what you're on about."

"My daughter has been abducted. Probably by your partner."

"I beg your pardon?"

"He's already threatened us with a gun – threatened

her with a gun."

"Now we're talking." Johnson's face twisted in pallid rage. "Now we're bloody talking. It was you who broke in here – you and your kids. I'm going to ring the police."

"You do that."

"Breaking and entering –"

"And you set those lads up to gas the badgers."

"I certainly did. They're bringing disease to my cattle."

"And planted Molotov cocktails on Andrews' premises."

"What rubbish are you talking now?"

"I found some more under your floorboards."

"With a gun?"

"Yes."

"I found them outside in the yard. I hid them in case I had to defend myself."

The lie was so ludicrous that Seb laughed. "Is this the Wild West?"

"Your friend Andrews is a dangerous vindictive man. Look what he did to your mill."

"He didn't do that."

"Who did?"

"*You* did." Losing control, Seb grabbed at his grubby-looking dressing-gown. "Where is she?"

"Leave me alone."

"Where *is* she?"

"If you let your daughter wander around at night . . ."

Seb shook Johnson hard. "She was guarding the

badgers you've been trying to kill. You're causing havoc up there, aren't you? Setting those engines up, kidnapping my daughter . . ."

"I own that land –"

"Yeah? I can prove otherwise. Remember what else there was under those boards?"

For the first time Johnson looked disconcerted. Seb could see the sweat standing out on his brow. Obviously he *had* forgotten what was hidden there.

"You were breaking –"

"Your friend took a few copies. I retained one, however. How the hell did you think you'd get away with it? By harassing Andrews, I suppose, so that he'd give up and sell the whole place to you at a give-away price. Now, for the final time, *where is she*?"

Johnson shrugged. "She's here. And we didn't abduct her. She was trespassing – and terrified. Being out at night like that on her own. Poor kid. Raymond brought her back here for her own protection.

"Now I've heard everything," said Seb.

"There's a door at the back," said Tim. "He must have gone out that way."

"OK. Let's take it quietly."

The door opened and they found themselves facing a grassy space that was bounded on three sides by parts of the engine shed and on the other by a derelict gate topped by barbed wire.

"Supposing they're having a go at the engines?" Tim couldn't think where they should be: here exploring, or on guard elsewhere.

"Hang on," said Brian. "I've got an idea. Maybe we should go back inside." He winked at Tim, quietly pointing to an old telephone box – just the kind of object Mr Andrews would collect. It was standing upright, but almost completely covered in foliage. Tim looked at it curiously and immediately saw what Brian must have noticed. There was a flattened area of grass outside it. The door must have been opened and closed very recently.

"This way. Oh, I don't need to show you, do I?" said Johnson. "You know your way already. Incidentally, I assume it was you who sent me on that wild goose chase?"

"I thought natural greed would prevail."

Johnson turned to him and Seb suddenly realized how desperate he was. He had a wild-eyed, hungry look to him. What the hell led you into all this, he wondered. Wife leaving? Farm going bust? Was it all bad enough for him to wage war on the vulnerable Mr Andrews? Was it bad enough to try to get his land? He supposed it was. In a way he felt sorry for Johnson – for having to recruit the sad young kids who had originally been Mr Andrews' protégés, for having to keep company with a man on the make like the pin-striped Harris.

"She's upstairs."

"I hope she's OK."

"She's fine. But you're not going to be. Not when you have to talk to the police."

"You'll be doing some explaining yourself," said Seb calmly. "In fact I'll welcome the chance of a talk with them." But inside he was anything but calm. What was happening to Tim and Brian? Maybe he should never have left them in such danger.

"Wait." Brian walked slowly but purposefully up to the telephone box. Quickly, he pulled open the door. A girl was crouching inside. But she had a knife.

"Blimey," was all Brian could say.

"Don't try anything," she said. The girl was small and only a couple of years older than them. She had long fair hair and a tired, grubby face.

"I recognize you," said Brian suddenly. "Didn't you sleep rough in the engineers' office at one time? Didn't Mr Andrews let you do that?"

"What if he did?"

"Funny way to repay him, messing about with his engines. And what about those cars? Got plans for them, have you?"

"Shut up."

"Why should I?"

She stood up, but this emphasized her fragility. If only it wasn't for the knife, thought Tim.

"So it was you who set all the engines moving?" he said in amazement.

"It's easy enough. Once you move them wooden blocks they just roll out."

"Don't you think that was a really rotten thing to do?" said Brian indignantly. "They're like family to Mr Andrews; they're precious to him. How could

101

you smash them all up? Don't you know he's in hospital – dying?"

She stared at him incredulously. "*What*?"

"He's very ill," amended Brian.

"Dying?"

"Maybe. If we can sort out this mess, maybe we can save him."

Without any warning, the girl burst into terrible dry sobs. There were no tears in her eyes. But the sobs convinced both Brian and Tim that she was genuinely in anguish.

"He won't die," she gasped. "He won't die, will he?"

"We told you the truth," said Brian starkly.

"He was good to me."

"Then why did you *do* this to him?" asked Tim. "*Why*?"

"It was just the money. I needed it."

"Who gave it to you? Johnson?"

She nodded. "And his partner. He's coming soon."

"Who?"

"Ray Harris. He's got a low-loader and a winch."

"What for?" asked Tim.

"The cars, stupid. In there. No one knew he'd got them until Harris started searching the place. Said they were worth a fortune."

"He's going to *steal* them?" asked Brian furiously.

"Yes."

"And you were going to let him?"

"I'm not now," she said with sudden composure.

"Why not?" asked Tim, thrown by her sudden change of heart.

"It didn't seem so bad before, but now I know Mr Andrews is ill in hospital we'll have to stop them."

"You mean it?" asked Brian suspiciously. "You mean you'll help us?"

"Of course I mean it."

"What's your name?" asked Tim doubtfully.

"Tina," she said.

"Dad –"

She was lying on the bed, her face smudged with dried tears.

"Flower – oh God – have they hurt you?"

But she was staring straight ahead, and at first he couldn't think what she was doing. Was she drugged? Or –. Then he realized and half turned, but too late to ward off the blow from the spanner Johnson had picked up from a chair outside the door. Seb fell forward, the darkness closing in on him and Flower's screams ringing in his ears. Then he knew nothing else.

"Listen."

They could hear it too: a rumbling sound from far off down the bottom of the track. It must be the low-loader coming.

"What are we going to do?" Tim asked Brian, but before he could reply Tina said, "We're going to catch him in the act."

"And then?"

"Jump him. Three of us should be able to keep him quiet."

Tim swallowed and Brian cleared his throat. Neither of them was sure. Harris had looked pretty tough at the farm.

"Then what?" asked Tim, trying to sound casual.

"We'll bung him in the cooler."

"What's that?"

"It's a little room Mr Andrews uses for keeping home-made wine. It's in a kind of cellar under the shed. I think he said it was used by the engineers."

Was there no end to Mr Andrews' hidey-holes, wondered Tim. Then he froze: the truck was almost at the gate.

"Get down," said Tina.

"Down? Where? There's nowhere to hide," hissed Brian.

"All right. Let's get in the telephone box."

"We'll never fit," whispered Tim.

"We'll have to," she said.

They all raced for the box at once as the truck stopped and the engine was switched off. For a few grisly seconds, it seemed that they were *not* going to fit in: at first they all remained jammed in the entrance. But, miraculously, the door closed and the foliage fell back across the glass in time, leaving a tiny peephole through which they could take it in turns to see the stocky figure of Ray Harris, looking odd without his pin-stripes, opening the gate and propping it back. It wasn't long before he began to reverse, slowly and cautiously, through the narrow aperture.

"Dad."

"Mm?"

"Dad!"

"God, my head."

"Are you all right?"

"No, I'm not." Seb opened his eyes to a blinding headache and the realization that he and Flower were tied together and then to the bed. Suddenly a dreadful thought slipped into his mind. "The documents –"

"He took them."

"No!"

"I'm sorry. I fought him but . . ."

"You're sure he took them?"

"Yes."

"Oh God, my head's splitting." He looked at Flower's face. One of her eyes was swollen and blackened. "Did he do that to you?"

"I tell you, I fought him, Dad."

"I'll –"

"*No*. I've scratched him. Deep. All down the side of his face. He's a marked man."

Seb grinned, and then frowned. "I have Luke and his mate tied up in the landrover. Let's hope he doesn't find them."

"He's dashed off somewhere."

"It's right off the main road."

They lay there without speaking for a moment.

Then Seb snapped, "OK. What are we waiting for?"

"I tried to get free. But no luck."

"It's just a question of . . ." He struggled. "Difficult, but not insurmountable." Seb struggled again. "This knot – if I can get at it with my teeth." Eventually he managed to wriggle himself down and then began to chew at the rope. After a while he surfaced, spluttering.

"Any progress?"

"Sure. It's going to be a long job." He twisted his wrist round so he could glance at his watch. "Six. What the hell is going on with Brian and Tim? I hope to God they're safe." He went back to the knot and didn't come up again for ages. When he did and was lying back panting, Flower asked anxiously, "Is it coming?"

"It will."

"What about your teeth?"

"It's a test, but I'll make it. Somehow. I'm only trying to prise the knot apart, not trying to bite through the rope." He gave a wry laugh. "After all, I'm not Superman."

"You could have fooled me," she replied.

"In a minute," whispered Tim. "Not yet."

They could see that the truck had been backed right up to the doors of the workshop. Harris must be somewhere inside, attaching a chain to one of the beautiful old cars.

Tina peered out again. She was an amazing

character: despite her diminutive size she had completely taken them over.

"Now!" She opened the door quietly and they followed her out. Tina beckoned them on. "When I say go, we rush him. Jump him. And pin him to the floor."

"Right," said Tim.

"OK," replied Brian. Both of them were feeling slightly sick.

There was a short pause that seemed like an eternity. Then Tina whispered, "Go."

"I can't do it."

"What?"

"I just can't do it. My teeth are giving me hell and I've made the knot so wet I can't get the last bit of it undone."

"Hang on, Dad, let me have a go."

"Can you see?"

By wriggling sideways, Flower could just see the resistant knot. "Right, here I go."

Slowly, she worked at the knot.

"Your teeth are smaller, sharper," said Seb appreciatively.

"You make me sound like a baby wolf," said Flower as she came up for air.

"How's the eye?"

"Painful."

"I'll kill him."

"You ought to see *his* face."

She buried her head again and continued to work

at the knot. Suddenly, she succeeded and it loosened.

"Dad –"

"Mm?"

"I've done it. I've done it!"

"Well done."

"I'll just finish off." Flower emerged triumphant. "I've done it. You can free your hands now."

Seb freed them and rubbed them together. Then he began to untie the remaining ropes.

"Where now?" she asked.

"Back to the battleground," he said.

Battleground it was. Harris, caught off guard, had gone down hard on the concrete floor as Tina neatly rugby-tackled him, and the two boys immediately leapt on his chest and legs. He swore and shouted and thrashed and swore again but to no avail; despite his considerable build and strength, they were too much for him. A few seconds later, Tina had the knife at his throat. "Move and I'll cut you."

"Get off."

"Lie still."

Tim was feeling dazed. A flailing foot had caught him in the mouth, but he hung on grimly.

"You damn kids!"

"Lie still," said Tina again. She had worked him over on to his stomach. "You're well and truly nicked."

"These cars are my property."

"Can you prove it?"

"Of course I can."

"They belong to Mr Andrews," said Brian. "The whole place does."

Suddenly the big man lay still. "Tina, you must be potty," he said quietly.

"Thanks."

"You don't know which side your bread's buttered. Do you?"

"I think I do."

"I can make it worth your while."

"Yeah?"

"You wouldn't be wanting."

"How much?"

For a horrible moment Brian and Tim thought she was going to bargain with him.

"If you let me up . . ."

"How much?"

"I reckon I can make it worth your while, Tina. I mean, I did before and I'll do it again."

She bounced up and down on Harris's back and he squealed with pain. "That's what I think of your offers."

"Tina."

But she bounced up and down again.

"Careful," said Brian.

"Eh?"

"You'll hurt him."

"See if I care," replied Tina.

"I do," said Harris piteously. "She's breaking my ribs."

"Then do as I say," she announced fiercely.

"I'll not –"

"Do as I say."

"What do you want?"

"Stand up. And if you try to run I'll get you. Understand?"

"Yes."

"Get up then."

"If you lot'll get off –"

"Get up."

They clambered off him and Harris rose slowly and unsteadily to his feet.

"This way."

"Where are we going?"

"Somewhere nice and comfy."

She prodded him with the knife and he lurched forward through the steel doors and into the engine shed. "Down the stairs."

"Where?"

"There."

She shoved him round the back of one of the two remaining locomotives and forced him to stumble down a short flight of iron steps.

"Go on."

"Where?"

"Go *on*." Tim was right behind Harris as she pushed him into the dark little room and clanged the door behind him. Then she drew across a rusty but effective bolt. His bullish face appeared at a tiny dusty window. "Tina!"

"Yeah."

"You don't know what you're missing out on, girl – messing me about like this. How about fifty?"

"I'm laughing."

"Seventy-five."

"Still laughing."

"A hundred."

"It's hilarious."

"A hundred and –"

"Now shut up!" She walked away as he was still trying to bargain with her. By the time she had joined the boys at the top of the steps Harris was up to a hundred and seventy-five and still counting.

"They're still here."

Flower peered into the dim interior of the land-rover. Seb removed the gags from Luke and his friend and a tirade of filthy language immediately followed.

"Now, now," said Seb. "Quieten down."

"What now?" asked Flower. "Straight back to Mr Andrews' yard?"

"Yes. I hope to God they're all right."

"There's a car out there," said Tim. "Round at the gate."

"Same treatment," replied Tina calmly.

"He got out, I think."

"Why didn't you tell me?"

"You were dealing with Harris," said Brian. Then he stopped. "Wait. Don't move."

It was Johnson. He was standing half in and half out of the steel shutter. There was a gun in his hand and he was pointing it at them. "Stay there."

"One hundred and ninety-five. Tina, I can't go

higher than that," echoed Harris's voice.

"What the hell's going on?" said Johnson. "Raymond!"

"Terry –"

"Yes?"

"Is that you, Terry?"

"Of course it bloody is. Where are you?"

"Them kids. They banged me up in here. Let me out!"

"You let a few kids –"

"She's got a knife."

Johnson's voice softened unpleasantly. "You turned traitor on us then, Tina darling?"

"Looks like it, doesn't it?" she replied truculently.

Tim felt sick with frustration and rage. Just when they looked like winning . . . Beside him Brian was stock still. Tim wondered what he was thinking.

"That was a very silly thing to do, darling. Have they laid some cash on you? I mean I know you always go to the highest bidder."

"Terry," came Harris's voice. "Terry –"

"Shut up a minute."

"Terry!"

"I said shut up. Let's have the knife, Tina love."

"No way."

"Knife please."

"I told you. No chance."

"If I shoot you . . ."

"You wouldn't have the bottle," she taunted him. "You little cow."

Suddenly Tim realized that Johnson was losing

control. His voice was shaking and his temper obviously rising.

"Naughty language," she scoffed.

"You –"

"Naughty temper."

"Tina, watch it," whispered Brian and Tim knew that he had also realized Johnson was on the edge. But Tina seemed oblivious.

"I'm not giving you no knife. You're just a wally, that's all."

The shot rang out with appalling clarity. Tim couldn't see where it caught her but it spun her round. She muttered something, and fell like a stone.

Johnson stared down at her. His eyes were like little black coals and they looked as if they had somehow shrunk back into his head.

"What's happening?" yelled Harris from below. "What's up, Terry?"

"You've killed her," said Brian as he darted over to Tina. She was on her face and there was blood coming from somewhere. An awful lot of it. She twitched and was still.

"Tina . . ."

"What's happening?" Harris kept yelling. "What's happening?"

Johnson still stood there, the gun in his hand. He looked totally glazed. Tim didn't know what to do. Was he going to kill them all? Then, unexpectedly, Johnson turned and walked stiffly away.

"Tim, Brian." It was Seb's voice.

Flower's voice shouted in to them too: "Are you in there? Brian? Tim?"

They froze. Johnson paused at the door and levelled the gun.

"Dad, don't come in," screamed Brian.

"He's got a gun," yelled Tim.

Slowly Johnson turned again. This time the gun was levelled at Tim.

"Don't move, Flower. Stay where you are."

"But –"

"I *said* don't move." Seb stood very still and spoke loudly, calmly, clearly. "Mr Johnson."

"Go to hell."

"I want you to put down that gun."

"I have it levelled at one of your kids."

"Put it down."

"I'm going to do for him."

"If you do, it'll be murder." Seb's voice was still amazingly calm. "Right now, this is a property dispute. Don't turn it into anything else."

"He's shot Tina, Dad."

"*What?*"

"Shut up!" said Johnson, his voice high and unsteady. "Just shut up."

"Who's Tina?"

"A girl we –"

"I said shut up!"

"Mr Johnson –"

"What is it?"

Flower's hopes rose. Would he start to talk to Dad?

"This girl Tina –"

"She's dead."

"Are you sure?"

"I killed her, didn't I?"

"And you're quite sure she's dead?"

"If she's not already, she soon will be." He gave a little giggle of hysterical laughter.

"You should check."

"I don't –"

"Now."

There was a long silence and neither Seb nor Flower could hear any movement.

"Mr Johnson –"

"The kid's checking."

"What's the –"

"Dad –" It was Brian.

"Yes?"

"Her heart's beating. I'm sure it's beating."

"Don't touch her."

"No."

"Johnson, I want you to come out. Drop the gun first."

"No chance."

"She'll die."

"So?"

"Work it out for yourself, man. You're escalating all this into bloody warfare. You *have* to come out."

"No."

"I'll call an ambulance and we'll get her clear."

"No."

"Then I'm coming in."

"If you do, I'll shoot this kid."

"I'm coming in." Seb was still steely calm. He took a step forward but Flower grabbed his arm.

"He means it," she hissed.

"I have to call his bluff."

"No."

"You come in, Mr Howard, and I'll kill another one."

"She's not *dead*." His voice broke.

"She soon will be." Johnson laughed mockingly. Then he said, "Don't move, son."

"What's happening?" yelled Seb, his voice breaking again. But no one told him.

"Don't move, son," Johnson repeated. "I warn you."

The shot thundered in the echo chamber of the engine shed.

Tim flung himself to one side while Brian shouted something that he couldn't understand. He lay on the hard concrete floor, curled up, as if back in the womb. Had he been hit? He certainly felt numb. Join Green Watch and die, he said to himself over and over again. Somewhere behind that insistent inner voice there was a thought pounding away: why had he ever got involved in the first place? He must have been crazy. Now this mad bloke had shot him. In cold blood. Dimly he could hear Brian shouting. What was he shouting about? Tim didn't want to know. He closed his eyes and rolled over. He was sure that he was getting more and more numb. And his heart was beating faster than it had ever beaten in his life. What the hell was he going to do? Well, he was going to die, wasn't he? He definitely hadn't got long. Tim opened his eyes. But only to check if there was any blood. He couldn't see any but that meant nothing and –

"You idiot."

"Eh?"

"Get up, you idiot."

"What?" How dare Brian speak to him like that. When he was dying. Didn't he even care?

"Get up."

"I'm shot," Tim croaked.

"You're not. He shot in the air. Now he's escaped." There were other voices but they were in the distance. "Dad's gone."

Tim got up with as much dignity as he could. "I thought I'd been shot," he said.

"Well, you haven't. Get moving. Dad's calling an ambulance for Tina."

Realizing what a fool he'd been, Tim got up and rushed over to Tina, but she was sitting up, clutching her arm.

"I don't know what you're all making such a fuss about," she said. "He's only nicked me."

"You sure?" asked Tim, certain that she must be lying and feeling very guilty.

"Course I'm sure. I fainted, didn't I? Just fainted," she added in disgust.

Flower nodded and laughed. "She's fine. And so are you, Tim."

"I feel an idiot."

"Don't." She came over to him and put her arm round his shoulders. "You were great, Tim. There's nothing to worry about." And he realized that there wasn't.

"It's all right."

Seb was standing in the copse with Flower as Brian and Tim ran up. The ambulance had already taken Tina and they could hear the siren of a police car.

"Where is he?" asked Brian.

"He emptied his bullets into the badger sett – down one of the holes."

"But –" Tim was amazed he was so calm. "Would he have hurt them . . .?"

"No chance." Seb was quietly reassuring. "Those tunnels are full of twists and turns. The bullets would never reach them."

"So what's he doing now?"

"He's clicking the trigger, and talking to himself."

"Gone potty?" asked Brian.

"No," said Flower. "Actually I think he's just in shock."

"I'll go to him now." Seb walked slowly across to Johnson and tapped him on his shoulder. "You've got something of Mr Andrews'. Hand it over now."

Johnson threw the gun to one side and Seb picked it up. "You know it's not the gun."

Johnson's hand went to his inside pocket and he pulled out the documents.

"Dad, he's going to tear the whole lot up," yelled Flower.

"No he's not," said Seb soothingly. He grabbed Johnson's wrist and, like the gun, he dropped the documents on the ground. Seb picked them up. It looked as if Johnson had completely given up. And when he spoke they all knew he had. "I've had it," he said.

"You've been a fool." Seb was his cold, angry self again and there was not a hint of compassion in his voice. "And you're going to have a lot of charges slung at you."

"They won't believe you," he said in a desperate attempt to regain some confidence. But with no success.

"They will. You shot Tina: that's attempted murder for a start. Then they'll see the low-loader and come across your mate Raymond safely locked up, and your pathetic little gang safely trussed up. That's quite a lot to be going on with."

"I can talk my way –"

"Can you?" Seb looked up towards the engine shed. Two policemen were hurrying down towards them.

Johnson turned back to the sett and waved his fist. "Those bloody things. They're vermin. And you know it."

"You know they're not. They were just an excuse, weren't they? Just another way of hassling Mr Andrews. You even co-opted the kids he tried to help."

119

"I'm broke. I needed that land to expand –"

"Sure. Save it for the judge."

Johnson tried to twist away from him but it was no good. Seb had his arm in a grip of iron.

"What shall we do with Harris, Dad?" asked Brian.

"Don't do anything. These gentlemen will deal with him."

"What's going on down here?" asked one of the policeman, hot and out of breath. "Apparently someone's been –"

"There's been a lot going on," said Seb. "Let me explain."

The explanation lasted a long time, during which Johnson said nothing.

"Do you deny all this?" asked one of the policemen eventually.

"I want to see my solicitor. I'm not saying anything," he whispered.

"Very well. You'd better come down to the station."

"Don't forget our friend in the engine shed."

The policeman grinned. "You've made a complete package of it, haven't you?"

Seb smiled. "It's been busy." He turned to Tim. "I've got to go down to the police station, but I know there's one place you want to be."

"The mill. Rusty?"

"I'm sure he's fine. But cycle back with Brian and just check." He turned back to the policeman.

"That's all right, isn't it, officer? Tim wants to check his dog's all right."

The policeman nodded. "Do that son. And then come down to the station. We've got quite a bit to sort out."

Although he was absolutely exhausted, Tim was glad to be allowed to check up on Rusty. Green Watch was amazing, he thought. No regular bedtime or meals; everyone accepting that they ate and slept when the work was done. What would Mum make of that, he wondered, and realized that he hadn't thought of her or Dad for quite a long time. Tim wasn't sure whether that was a good thing or not; he just knew that Seb and Green Watch had filled his life to such an extent that there was little room for anything else.

The windmill was intact, and so was Rusty. He rushed up to Tim and Brian as soon as they opened the gate.

"Good boy," said Tim, gathering the big dog up in his arms. He looked round at the half-completed stockade. "We're not going to need this, are we? All these defences?"

"You never know," said Brian. "Maybe we should finish building it. Green Watch has never been very popular."

"Do you have a lot of enemies?" asked Tim as Rusty bounded and barked around him.

"Well, what we do isn't always very popular, but

we have to go on doing it." He sounded very calm and matter of fact.

"Brian –" Tim was suddenly hesitant.

"Yes?"

"Can I belong to Green Watch?"

"You already do."

"But suppose you go abroad. Something exciting. Could I come too?"

"If your parents agree."

"What about Seb?"

"Oh, he'd take you like a shot."

"Really?"

"Tim, don't you realize?"

"Realize what?"

"You've proved yourself."

Tim thought of himself lying on the floor of the engine shed, convinced he had been shot. When he hadn't. And Tina had. He thought he was a bit of a coward really. "You sure?"

"Course I'm sure. Tim, you're in Green Watch – whether you like it or not."

But Tim did like it.

Epilogue
Two weeks later

They were as still as sentinels as they waited for the badgers. Seb, Flower, Brian and Tim. Mr Andrews was there too, leaning on a stick, having defied the hospital authorities about being out at night. Beside him stood Tina with her arm in a sling. Half an hour later they were rewarded as the badgers came out, the young playing and the elders first watching, then drifting quietly off to hunt.

On the way back to the caravan Seb put his arm through Mr Andrews'. "How do you feel?"

"I'm great, but I wouldn't be if it wasn't for you and Green Watch. And Tina. By the way, I think she's got a request."

Tina spoke abruptly as if she didn't really care. But they all knew she did. "This Green Watch rubbish."

"Yes?" Seb was grinning.

"Can anyone join? Or is it just for you lot?"

"We've already got one new member. Tim here."

"So membership's closed – even for honorary members," she snapped and gave a half-sneering, half-nervous laugh.

"Did I say that?"

"Well –"

Seb turned to the others. "Do you reckon Tina's a suitable member for Green Watch?"

"Course you don't," she scoffed.

"Course we do," chorused the others.

"You mean it?"

"I mean it," said Seb. "We all mean it. Like Tim, you proved yourself. So do you want to join?"

"Don't mind if I do," she mumbled. Tim could see there were tears in her eyes. "Shan't have much time to actually do anything if I'm looking after him," she smiled at Mr Andrews. "But it'd be great to be a member."

Mr Andrews turned round and looked back at the copse in the moonlight. "That's what it's all about," he said.

"What's that?" Seb looked at him curiously.

"It's about freedom," said Mr Andrews. "Freedom for the badgers – and me – and the cars and the engines. And I never realized I had it already. I keep that paper on me now. And I've copied it twelve times."

"Even with it, you wouldn't have had that freedom. There was always Johnson – and his desperation."

"But that's what I mean," replied Mr Andrews. "That's what Green Watch stands for, isn't it? Sticking up for freedom."

"Yes," said Seb slowly. "It's a good motto, isn't it? I think we should adopt it. Sticking up for freedom – with Green Watch."

They walked on towards the caravan. Tim wondered if the fantastic glow of elation was in everyone else's heart as well as his own. And when he looked at them all, he knew it was.